Johan du Toit grew up in a remote community, eight hours' drive north of Cape Town in South Africa. He immigrated to Australia with his family in 1994. Through membership of a writers' group, Johan found an opportunity to write short fiction. In 2022 *Meandering Road*, a collection of his short stories, was produced by Broadcast Books and published independently. Johan lives with his wife in Sydney.

Also by Johan du Toit
Meandering Road: Stories inspired by images, travel and life experiences across continents

When only today matters

and other stories

JOHAN DU TOIT

BROADCAST

The stories in this collection are works of fiction, although some places, events and names are real.

First published in Australia in 2025 by Johan du Toit
johan.dutoit7b@gmail.com

A catalogue record for this work is available from the National Library of Australia

ISBN: 978 0 6458440 9 2 (Paperback)
ISBN: 978 1 7638250 0 0 (Ebook)

Produced by Broadcast Books, www.broadcastbooks.com.au
Edited by Peter Vaughan-Reid and Bernadette Foley
Proofread by Puddingburn Publishing Services
Cover design by Christa Moffitt, Christabelladesigns
Typeset in Garamond Premier Pro 12.5/17pt by Matthew Oswald, Like Design
Cover photograph: iStockphoto, tomeng
Author photograph by Hoa-an Bratland
Printed by IngramSpark

Johan du Toit and Broadcast Books acknowledge that Aboriginal and Torres Strait Islander peoples are the Traditional Custodians and the first storytellers of the lands on which we live and work.

Contents

Preface

The characters and their individual journeys in *When Only Today Matters and Other Stories* were all inspired by pictures. This quest of finding characters with a story worth telling started some sixteen years ago, when I joined a writers' group in Sydney. We have averaged four rounds of storytelling every year since inception, with the winner in an anonymous vote enjoying the privilege of choosing a picture for the next round.

With the passing of time, and some encouragement from an acclaimed author, I have explored the lives of two characters without the restriction of the word count set by the writers' group. In the story 'When Only Today Matters', the corporate lawyer who sacrifices his career and eventually his family, is based on a personal experience as a volunteer on Christmas Day at the Wayside Chapel in Sydney's Kings Cross. The journey of Rebecca in 'Shadow of the Flat Top Mountain' is a reflection on real-life trauma under the apartheid regime in

South Africa, the way I remember it.

The eight stories chosen for this collection were shaped by my personal journey. While it always started with a picture, the human truth element came from a place of gratitude or a sense that tomorrow may be a better day.

The stories with a whisper of hope include the teenage boy who challenges his father's recollection of history, and the goatherd's encounter in the desert with two women praying together in spite of a deep religious divide.

Then there are stories fuelled by injustice and frustration. The student activist whose crime was the colour of his skin, or the young man forced to fight a war he didn't believe in, far from home.

We have chosen to include my first poem, 'Hear my Heart Whisper' to close the book. The poem recalls a childhood in a remote farming community.

Following our successful collaboration on *Meandering Road,* I have been fortunate to work with Bernadette Foley at Broadcast Books on the editing and publication of *When Only Today Matters and Other Stories.* Without Bernadette's wisdom and encouragement this would not have been possible. Forever grateful.

Uncle Wayne

I leave the raspberry jelly with water-thin custard untouched, someone in the kitchen may fancy my desert. After the hospital meal I feel bloated and uncomfortable, going to the toilet is painful. I mean the fact that I can't go by myself, always a nurse with a helping hand. At least they let me wipe myself.

The surgeon was honest, straight as an arrow.

'Wayne,' he said, 'we've taken out as much as we could. You need to learn how to live with half a stomach. You'll be in hospital for another three to four weeks, maybe a bit longer. We'll help you with your new diet, you need to chew until the food feels like paste in your mouth and, Wayne, you need to come off the booze.'

My first response was, I'm going to live a bit longer, but I can't imagine life without a settler. I was relieved the second bed in my ward was empty when the nurse with the purple rose tattoo on her wrist wheeled me in here and opened the blinds to a cloudless sky. I need time to think, in my own space, figure out what to do with my shaking hand. When the day moves towards sunset, what to reach out for, without the bottle, what else may help to sooth the loneliness.

Raelene left in a hurry, after thirty-two years. I didn't see this coming. Truth is I expected our life together on the property to last forever. She packed the car while I was out branding the steers. When I came home, ready for a cooked dinner, all I found was the letter. Just two paragraphs. Like a sniper, she didn't miss. I was a selfish, grumpy bastard with a drinking problem, she deserved better, still a life to live, new horizons, without me.

First the dull, pulsing cramp was manageable. Then came an excruciating pain, further down near the buckle of my belt, blood in the toilet, blood in my vomit on the front veranda. The doctor's first question was for how long? He meant the bleeding. When I said probably a couple of months, he picked up the phone and called the ambulance.

✦

I am struggling with the crossword in the *Telegraph* when the same nurse, with the tattoo, walks into my room. Without even a 'Good day', she announces in her shrill voice, 'Wayne, you've got company.'

Behind her an orderly in a green gown pushes a bed into my private space. I'm pissed off, but I don't say anything, to the nurse, the orderly or the patient who looks at me with big, dark eyes under the bandage around his head. The eyes send a smile before the boy raises his right hand off the white blanket to wave at me.

I offer him a nod before the nurse calls out, 'This is your roommate Luca.'

With our feet now facing in the same direction, the boy lies a few short steps away. Close enough for me to hear him breathe to the same rhythm as the machine on the other side of his bed. The nurse holds the boy's right hand as she stands between our beds. She has decided we'll get on well as roommates, and she says so, with the further comment that we don't really have much choice.

I want to use the nurse as a witness. After clearing the ever-present phlegm in my throat, I say, 'G'day, mate. Just to let you know I won't be much company. I prefer minding my own business.'

The boy nods, there is an awkward silence before the nurse says, 'Seriously, Wayne, you are an even bigger arsehole than I thought.'

She turns her back to me and helps the boy to sit up, resting against his two pillows.

After lunch, when the trays with our leftovers have been removed, I lie with my back to the boy, pretending to drift into an afternoon slumber. My self-imposed privacy hangs heavy in the room. The verdict from the nurse stays with me, it is hurtful because it is true.

Behind me I hear the boy's voice, softly as if he isn't sure whether I am asleep. 'Uncle Wayne.' Then again, this time louder. 'Uncle Wayne, are you having a day nap?'

My first reaction is a silent 'For fuck's sake' before I say, 'I was trying to get some rest.'

The boy doesn't apologise, instead he asks whether I play bingo. This is a game I know, Raelene and I had long, silent evenings to fill on the farm.

I mumble, 'Yes, but only once I've had a rest' and pull the white sheet up over my ear.

The squeaky wheel of the tea trolley wakes me, and I push myself, one inch at a time, into a sitting position. After soaking a Marie biscuit in my lukewarm tea, I notice the boy Luca is drinking milk through a straw from a plastic cup.

'Uncle Wayne, time for a game of bingo,' he calls out while I am still sucking on my Marie biscuit.

I'm thinking, Bloody hell, this kid is not going to leave me alone.

'Mate, one round only,' and I follow up with a deep sigh.

He is a little operator, this boy. With a sad, pleading face he convinces the guy fetching the tea trays to leave the trolley between our beds. 'Uncle Wayne and I are going to play bingo and you know, we're not allowed out of our beds.'

Luca's mother and father, an Italian couple with a vegetable farm near Windsor as Luca had proudly told me earlier, visit him that evening. He is excited to see them and introduces me as 'Uncle Wayne, my roommate.'

They come across as courteous, they smile but their eyes show a darker helplessness. After they draw the curtain between our two beds I hear whispering conversations, interrupted by long moments of silence. Luca is asleep by the time they leave, the father with his arm around his wife's shoulder. In the bed next to me lies their curious boy, eight on his next birthday he'd said during the bingo, and behind that bandage around his head hides a creeping monster he cannot see.

My roommate wakes every morning with the excitement of new possibilities. Cheerful and chatty, he makes me feel mine may be a half-decent day after all. Ready to unpack the Lego as soon as the doctor has made his rounds, he imagines skyscrapers with blue Perspex panels as windows and fits cantilever floors into his buildings, in his favourite colour yellow.

I am holding back, but after watching his project taking shape, I suggest he should perhaps consider green gardens around those tall buildings.

'Good idea, Uncle Wayne, where they can have picnics with their families.'

After morning tea, he cleverly drags me into a round of bingo, and then a drawn-out game of Monopoly. When I say, 'Mate, I'm feeling a little buggered', Luca can't hide his disappointment but keeps himself busy colouring in page after page in the thick book that usually sits on his bedside table.

As the days go by my reluctance wanes. Without one of my own I could not have imagined the joy this child's smile brings to my miserable life. Most mornings I wake when it's still dark outside our window, waiting for Luca to stir, to call my name.

We play, unaware of the age difference. Occasionally he lets me win in bingo, we laugh, he finds jokes about farts very funny. I tell him ghost stories, he wants to hear graphic detail of how a calf is born. I demonstrate its wobbly first steps.

There are days when the nurse with the rose tattoo, her name badge says 'Elize', reminds me I am a very sick patient, to take it easy.

During my daily blood pressure test Elize leans closer and says there will be a second operation. I nod but I don't ask when.

✦

As the orderly behind a blue face mask pushes Luca's bed towards the door I shout, 'See you later, mate.' The boy responds with a thumbs-up before his head with the white bandage disappears down the wide corridor.

I fight the sleep, listening for the wheels of his bed. Eventually my eyes become too heavy.

Elize is next to my bed at first light, her long fingers resting on my forearm. The second bed is empty, made up with fresh white linen.

'Why not me, Elize?' I ask. 'What have I ever done?'

'Probably more than you know, Wayne. He is desperately ill, fighting for his life, but in this room, Luca has made a new friend.'

Together we cry in silence, before the nurse says, 'Wayne you should look after this.' She leaves Luca's colouring-in book on my bed.

After an empty stare at nothing, I open the book. Inside the front cover, on a blank page, there is a drawing of a smiling face with wrinkles like a dried prune. Above the old man's face, Luca had written with rounded letters, 'Uncle Wayne not so grumpy.'

When Only Today Matters

Level 42, George Street, Sydney

There is half an hour before the partners' meeting and I have given my personal assistant a clear instruction to hold all calls. I feel entitled to this moment of reflection.

From my corner office, I have an unobstructed view of the Harbour Bridge. I swivel my chair; I can now see Cockatoo Island and beyond the Balmain peninsula to the hazy blue of the mountains. As I continue my slow merry-go-round I appreciate the oil on canvas landscape on the wall behind my chair. On the antique desk to my right stands a framed black and white profile photograph of our daughter Chloe, a gift from her on my forty-fifth birthday last November.

I think about the first eighteen years of my life in Balmain, our one-up terrace house on Duke Street, an address my dad referred to as 'a little bit posh'. That leads me to think about Dad's reminder never to address my friends as 'youse'; he said that to me on the night before the ambulance took him away.

Dad was a tall clean-shaven man with honey blond hair that he combed backwards without a parting. I remember the strength in his arms as he lifted me on his shoulders for a better view of the Australia Day regatta on the harbour. He found a job at Arnott's when he left school without completing his HSC, but that didn't hold him back. By the time the doctor signed his early retirement letter, Dad was the dispatch manager, in charge of those red trucks that delivered biscuits all over Sydney. When Mum and I saw an Arnott's truck on Darling Street we would stop to wave, even though we didn't know the driver. That's how I want to remember him, not the old man with the sunken eyes who the two men in blue uniforms wheeled out to the ambulance. I waited for him on the front steps, even after Mum said, 'He is gone now, David.'

Those early years were compartmentalised by my progress towards a proper education. I started at Balmain Public up the road. My mother took on a second shift at the hospital to put me through Riverview, a private boys' school with grounds like a public park. The final leg of the journey ended in the Great Hall at Sydney University, my mother in a pale yellow dress, sitting in the second row, wiping a tear with her cotton handkerchief as the chancellor tapped me gently on the head.

By then Mum and I were not close anymore, beyond birthdays we had little contact. The reason for this separation was a man called Trevor Cleary, who moved into our house when some of Dad's clothes were still hanging in the wardrobe of our spare bedroom. Mum was lonely, vulnerable and this man grabbed his opportunity. When my mother was at work Cleary spent his days drinking and playing cards at The Royal Oak.

While we grew apart, I was motivated by my mother's aspiration for me. From here in my office on the partners' level, I can look back on my life knowing she would be immensely proud that I was able to escape our working-class neighbourhood. A partner at a Top-four law firm may even have been beyond her dreams for her only child.

Late this afternoon Jennifer will come into my office. We'll celebrate my new status as merger and acquisition partner at Pattersons with a glass of champagne. Jennifer will love the sound of crystal on crystal when we toast to having arrived.

The silence in my office suite is interrupted by a louder than usual ping from my phone; a reminder the meeting in the Macquarie Room is due to start in fifteen minutes. I lean forward to rest my elbows on the desk, my iPad shows the agenda for the meeting. Suddenly a little worm of uncertainty slithers into my chest.

Wynyard Park

It is just after 9.30 on Tuesday, the appointment with the chairman and chief executive of our telecommunications client was scheduled for 11 am. The park above Wynyard Station is normally a busy corridor in the city. I desperately need to be on my own and I'm relieved to see a vacant bench in a sunny spot.

Last night I was in the office until after midnight. My team ordered pizzas for dinner, and I sent them home at around ten o'clock to allow me time for a final review of the document. The next day's meeting was critical in confirming my client's acquisition bid. Staying back on my own was a mistake.

I found myself reading the same paragraphs over and over. I made revisions to the executive summary, but when I checked it against the supporting documentation I couldn't make the connection. I started doubting myself. When I leant back in my chair to rest my eyes for a few minutes, I drifted off. I looked at the screen again; the cursor was flashing where I'd deleted text, but I struggled to remember what and why. The only option was not to save the changes.

In bed this morning, I turned over and fell asleep after Jennifer left for her yoga class. By the time I was dressed the car had been waiting outside the house for 20 minutes and I didn't have time for breakfast. The traffic down William Street into the city seemed heavier than usual; in response to my 'Bugger' the driver said something about an earlier accident on Elizabeth Street.

Going up in the packed lift I wiped the perspiration off my upper lip and pulled down my tie to undo the top button of my shirt. My team of four lawyers were already waiting in the Bligh Room for the final review, but instead I walked to the partners' wing where my assistant Rowena stood as I opened the door. I noticed the frown when I instructed her to reschedule the client meeting.

'Are you sure, David? This is very short notice.'

'Please, just do it, tell them we need more time.'

I felt uncomfortable about my abrupt tone, but without further explanation I walked into my office and closed the door. I sat down on the small couch, the silence in the room rang like a siren in my ears.

When I walked past her desk I said I should be back in an hour's time. Once downstairs on George Street I realised I didn't have my phone, but I kept walking. I avoided eye contact with the man at the Bridge Street intersection who held up a handwritten message on cardboard that said, 'Please help me, I am hungry.'

Alone on the bench in Wynyard Park now, I am wondering how the client will react to the late cancellation of the meeting. My comment, 'we need more time', will harm their confidence in my ability to handle such a complex deal. Those in my team, all smart young lawyers, will know that it's a bullshit excuse. This will be raised at the next partners' meeting; I'll need to come up with a credible reason for putting the firm's reputation at risk.

Intermezzo on Martin Place

Across the table with the starched white cloth and the small flickering candle, Jennifer swirls the pinot noir in her stemmed wine glass before bringing it up to her nose.

'To your incredible year, David, the front page of the *Financial Review* says it all, the new M&A Superstar.'

With the wine glass in the air, her eyes sweep around the busy Intermezzo restaurant.

'I spoke to Dad this afternoon and he asked that I pass on his congratulations.'

'Thank you, I appreciate that.' I hope Jennifer will move on from my award, especially as she seems to be speaking louder than usual.

'And you know what Mum's like, she will be dining out on her son-in-law's achievement.'

I smile briefly and suggest we should look at the menu. We decide to share the caprese salad with three varieties of tomato, followed by the slow cooked shoulder of lamb from the Riverina.

I have been delaying this moment for a couple of months now. Last night at the kitchen table the words bounced around in my mouth, like a sour plum. Then Jennifer's phone rang, it was Chloe. I couldn't help but to share in the excitement of her news. Our 'baby girl' accepted at NIDA with a full scholarship, on her way to becoming an actress.

With the salad finished, Jennifer uses a piece of sourdough bread to wipe the olive oil from her plate. She tilts her head to the side.

'David Anderson, I've been doing most of the talking tonight. Are you okay?'

I pick up my glass in search of courage.

'There's something you should know, a situation at work.' I pause, concentrating on my breathing.

'Let me guess, you've been approached by another firm?'

For a moment it seems as if the other diners have gone silent. Under the table I can feel my right leg jumping like a jackhammer.

'No. The truth is, I'm struggling at work.'

'What do you mean by struggling? Is it the workload? You look tired.'

'No, it's more than that, Jen. The responsibility and the clients' expectations, it's all getting to me.'

She leans forward with a frown; my wife seems intrigued.

'The only way I can get through the day, and I mean every day, is with my little helpers.'

'A little tablet won't do you any harm.'

Jennifer at least has the awareness to lower her voice, her fingers touch my hand holding the wine glass.

'I've been on pretty strong medication for months.'

'And you haven't mentioned any of this before?' she said.

I look down at my empty plate.

'Some days, and late nights at the office, I need more than the prescription medicine.'

Home alone in Woollahra

The yellow glow of the streetlight is sneaking through the plantation shutters. My shoes are on the floor next to the armchair, my feet rest on the leather ottoman. I hear the key in the front door. Jennifer walks into the semi-darkness of the lounge room and turns on the lights.

'Jesus, David, you scared the shit out of me.'

'I'm sorry.'

'What the hell are you doing at home this early?' Her tone is annoyed rather than concerned.

'It's getting dark already.' I realise immediately that it's a feeble response.

'Come on. Since when have you become a nine-to-fiver?'

'It's over, Jen.' I hope she will notice my exhaustion.

'The BMP takeover deal?' She walks further into the lounge room.

I need to take a very deep breath.

'No, I mean it really is all over. I just can't continue with this.'

'What? You're withdrawing from the transaction after all these months? For Christ's sake, David, tell me what's going on.'

I see a hint of a smile. She thinks I am playing the fool.

In a voice that must be barely audible, I tell her that I walked out of Pattersons earlier this afternoon.

'Jen, I can't do it anymore. I'm scared.'

'Scared of what?' she asks, pacing the room. 'This is bullshit!'

'It's over, Jen.'

'Stop saying it's over. What the hell does that mean?'

'It means that I'm not going back to the law firm. Tonight I'll send an email to the managing partner.'

'You've got to be kidding, David!' She comes closer to where I am sitting.

'What about this house and the deposit on the place in Byron? What do I say to my father?'

I realise my silence is fuelling her anger, but I don't know what to say.

'Tomorrow morning you'll get off your arse and back to the office.'

Centennial Park

For close on four years John Park, whose real name is Park Sung-Jin, has driven me between our home in Woollahra and my office in the city. On the last beep of the 7 am news on the radio, he navigates the bend approaching Oxford Street and looks at me in the rear-view mirror. For the third consecutive morning, I direct him to turn left to Centennial Park.

In the park John drives carefully past cyclists in bright vests as we circle round to the cafe in the centre of the park. We agree that he will pick me up at the same spot at 6.30 that evening. Stepping out of the Mercedes, I turn my face towards the autumn sun. The steel grip in my stomach unwinds, one twist at a time. I walk towards the evergreen oak beyond the duck pond. Ahead of me lies eleven hours of nothing, no meetings, no clients, no expectation.

✦

The light is fading and there is a cold breeze from the west. I turn up the collar of my suit jacket as I make my way along Grand Drive to the cafe, now shut for the night. As arranged, John Park is standing next to his black car with the tinted windows. It is only when he opens the door for me to slide into the back that I see Jennifer in the front passenger seat.

Not a single word is spoken during the ten-minute drive back to Jersey Road, John has turned the radio off. I feel no anger towards the loyal driver, no frustration that Jennifer has discovered my little secret, no blame for whoever reported my absence from the office. They will be hurting from the client's decision to engage another firm.

Back in the house, Jennifer calmly closes the front door. During the drive home, I have been preparing for a confrontation. Without a word she walks down the hall, and I follow like a puppy dog. In the kitchen she fills a tall glass with cold water from the dispenser on the fridge door. She drinks half in two long gulps. By the time she turns around, her face has grown ugly.

My wife makes every word count. I offer nothing in reply. She lifts her hand and I expect a blow. Instead, she looks at me in disgust, and with a voice that I don't recognise she says, 'You're a fucking loser, get out of here.'

She slams our bedroom door behind her, and I sit down on a chair at the kitchen counter. I feel relieved that I no longer have to live a lie, but I am uncertain what to do next. I can walk through the front door now, but where would I go?

After staring at nothing for a while I walk over and open the fridge door, but I am not hungry. So I go down the passage to the bedrooms, the last door on the left is Chloe's room. In the darkness I find the bed and remove my shoes.

'Get out of here,' Jennifer had screamed. That's what I'll do in the morning. Where I'll go is not clear. I roll on my side, a sharp stabbing pain behind my eyes, I feel exhausted, the sleep doesn't come. The digital clock on Chloe's bedside table glows bright red, 17 minutes after 2. In the pocket of my trousers my hand finds the strip of silver foil; there are two tablets left. It must be raining gently; I can hear water dripping from the gutter. I need to get someone in to fix it, but why am I worrying about that now?

Rushcutters Bay

On our evening drives home from the city John Park and I would pass a block of serviced apartments on New South Head Road in Rushcutters Bay. From the back seat I often wondered about the people who would choose to live in a place like that. A square concrete box with a flat roof, blacked-out windows that don't open, fake plants in two large flower boxes on either side of the revolving front door, a vertical neon sign flashing 'Vacancy' in green letters.

When I call for a taxi, this is the only address I can think of. Jennifer had left for work without saying goodbye. On a shelf in the garage, I found a backpack in which I stuff grey track pants and a pair of jeans, I count underpants for seven days and a pile of t-shirts, one with long sleeves. In the bathroom I keep a travel bag with essential toiletries including a packet of Panadol, which I add to my packing. On my way to the front door, I take my navy ski jacket from the hallway cupboard.

The woman at reception looks at me over the black-rimmed glasses resting on her longish nose and asks for my driver's licence and a credit card. She doesn't make me feel welcome, but she says so anyway. Because I am paying for a full month in advance she allocates me 'one of our popular studios with a park view'. I shake my head when she asks whether I have any other luggage.

I don't expect to hear from Jennifer until later in the afternoon. When she gets home she will see my letter in a white envelope on the floor just inside the front door. I didn't say where I was going because I didn't know, but she will try my mobile number.

It is dark outside when the phone rings, it's Jennifer's number but instead I hear Chloe's voice. 'Hello, Dad.'

When she asks where I am, I tell a lie. 'A hotel in the city, Chloe. '

'For how long, is this for business?' Jennifer has clearly not told her the full story.

'I'll be here for the rest of the week.' I want to keep this short but at the same time I'm hoping she won't simply say goodbye.

'Dad, is there a problem between you and Mum?'

'I don't think so. I just have a few issues to sort out at work.'

'You have my number, so please let me know when you're back at home.'

'I'll keep in touch.' The lies make me feel uncomfortable, but what else could I say?

I stare at my phone after Chloe has said goodbye. My home screen is a photo of her and Jennifer against the backdrop of the Cape Byron lighthouse, waving to the camera. I turn off the bedside lamp and push my face into the pillow. Next to me on the bed my phone vibrates. It is a text message from Jennifer.

'You didn't even have the courage to tell your daughter the truth. You are a disgrace to your family. My poor parents, the embarrassment they have to deal with. Dad's immediate reaction was that he should never have given his blessing.'

✦

After three days in bed with restless sleep and room service for dinner, I have a shower and change into clean clothes. I put on track pants and the long sleeve black t-shirt. I straighten the sheets, smooth out the beige bed cover and swap the two pillows. As I pull the chord of the vertical blind a streak of sunshine lights up the room. It is mid-morning. In the park leading down to Rushcutters Bay two small brown dogs chase a tennis ball. A woman in a red dress and white sneakers runs after them.

Over at the cafe most of the outside tables are occupied. I imagine the taste of a macchiato but sit down on the two-seater couch and turn on the television instead. After flicking through all the movie options I decide on an Oscar nomination, *The Chicago 7*, which Jennifer and I planned to see but we never made it to the cinema. I was probably working on a big deal at the time.

I wake up, my eyes heavy, still sitting on the couch with the remote in my hand, the film has just finished, with white titles on a black screen running through the names of the cast. My watch shows the time as just before midday. I know that isn't quite right because for years now I've set my watch at ten minutes early.

I switch off the television and stare at the black screen. The sun has moved away from my window, but there is still no need to turn on the overhead light. I slide down on the couch and put a small green pillow, the same colour as the receptionist's uniform, behind my neck.

The couch is uncomfortable, forcing me to shift position. At the law firm my former partners will be cleaning up the mess, in damage control. Jennifer would have made up her mind, with the support of her parents, Richard and Gretel won't tolerate a quitter in their family. After the first call not another word from Chloe, they would have got to her by now. Jennifer is right, I am a disgrace to my family, a marriage of twenty-two years, dropped like a plate on a concrete floor. I've paid for a full month's accommodation in this room with the worn brown carpet, this gives me time, but time for what? Why will another four weeks in this shithole make any difference? With a mouldy smell in my nostrils I decide, this will be my last night staying here. I come up with a plan, not for the rest of my life, but for tomorrow at least, I shall ask the woman at reception for resident access to a computer. The money should be in Chloe's saving's account the following day. I shall leave the key in the room and remove the 'Do not disturb' card from the door handle. Then I can walk through the revolving door downstairs, with the pack on my back, a deep breath of fresh air and no destination in mind.

Central Station

The kookaburras wake me at first light with their enthusiasm for the new day. After folding my sleeping bag into the backpack, I make my way from the tree in The Domain to Hyde Park, to wash my face in the fountain. Near the cafe behind St James Station, I watch from a safe distance as a young woman in a navy business suit looks at her phone and walks off in a hurry. In her paper cup she has left two decent sips of black coffee.

Ahead of me awaits a full day with an empty calendar. During the night the chill of the autumn dew had crept through my jeans and old ski jacket. But walking down Elizabeth Street the warmth of the sun on my back lifts my spirits, step by step.

Even as a relative newcomer, I recognise a few familiar faces outside the station entrance on Elizabeth Street. Nathan, a bald bloke with a crutch, has a fresh bandage around his leg this morning. He is in animated conversation with Geraldine, a skinny young woman wearing an oversized green waterproof jacket, and he doesn't take any notice of me. But Arthur calls out, 'G'day, David,' and with a pat of his palm invites me to join him on the pile of flattened cardboard boxes.

Arthur and I watch as a short bloke with bandy legs just makes it across the pedestrian crossing before the roar from a line of impatient cars. He walks briskly without any baggage.

'That's old mate Benny, but he doesn't normally hang around this part of town.' Arthur waves but Benny heads over to where Nathan and Geraldine lean against the station wall.

Under a well-worn Resch's Draught cap, Arthur's blue eyes are watery and his grey beard grows like tumbleweed. It is difficult to judge his age, but I would say early sixties or perhaps younger. It's my fourth day with Arthur. He tells me how he moved from Wagga to Sydney, he blames himself for his younger brother's death. Next August it will be eleven years. I don't mention that he has told me this sad story before.

'Mate, I always drove like a man with his arse on fire. Jesus, I saw the light of the freight train but thought we could make it through the crossing in time.'

The best part of a conversation with Arthur is that he doesn't expect you to say anything in response, as long as he can see you nodding. After a couple of hours, maybe more, Arthur decides it's time we find something to eat. He struggles to his feet, and we walk into Central Station. I let him walk ahead. Hunger is another new experience, but I still feel a little uncomfortable asking for food.

Arthur knows his dining options around the Grand Concourse. Shortly after lunch there will be generosity from the staff at Central Deli. There is no need to ask, we just hover near the double glass doors.

It is a busy day at the station; I am not sure whether it is Monday or Tuesday. After close to an hour our patience is rewarded when a bald man in a striped green and yellow waistcoat opens the door and holds out a brown paper bag with a cheerful, 'There you are, fellas, enjoy.' The round lapel button with a smiley symbol introduces him as 'LEONARD – MANAGER'.

Just inside the entrance from Pitt Street we find an unoccupied wooden bench. Arthur takes three sandwiches wrapped in cellophane from the paper bag and a couple of bruised red apples that wouldn't make it to the following day. There are two beef and pickle sandwiches with thick slices of meat and a cheese and tomato that we share. We eat in silence, except for Arthur's 'Bloody delicious' after his first bite of the beef and pickle on brown bread.

After lunch I thank Arthur for sharing the meal and walk slowly across the Grand Concourse back to the Elizabeth Street entrance. At the big electronic board passengers search for the names of stations on the suburban lines. A pregnant woman with her toddler fast asleep in a pram moves away when I stop close to them.

It is a pleasant day outside with a few lazy clouds, just a slight breeze from the south. I wave to Nathan who is now on his own, sitting on the pile of cardboard boxes with his crutch leaning against the sandstone wall of the station building. He doesn't respond and I realise he is having a nap. It takes a while for the lights to change, but I remind myself that I'm not in a hurry. Eventually I follow a stream of pedestrians across the intersection and make my way up Foveaux Street. I glance across to the silver roller door that is always shut. While it looks more like a car repair workshop the sign above the door shows a large dollar sign next to the words, 'THE TAX MAN'. I wonder who the customers for such a business may be around here. Or is it just a front for a money-laundering operation? Anyway, it is none of my business and I continue up the gentle hill.

Cooper Street Reserve

The little haven of green with beds of bright flowers is hardly a reserve, more like a suburban garden at the end of a cul-de-sac. It is peaceful, I am only vaguely aware of the steady drone of city traffic, and there's little chance anybody will disturb me on a weekday with uninvited conversation. Behind a hedge is the wooden wall of a childcare centre. I enjoy listening to the voices of the children as they spend their days away from home in a safe space. Sometimes I hear them crying for their mummies.

At the far end of the reserve is a one-way street with renovated terrace houses, their ground-floor windows protected by heavy steel bars. Next to the only gate a brown board with white letters warns that 'Camping or lighting fires is not allowed, penalties apply'. I think it is a polite way of saying that homeless people are not allowed in the reserve after dark, when the owners of those houses return from their day at work.

The bench I have claimed as my spot is half-hidden in the corner behind a white oak. I am about to settle in for a nap when a bloke with two suitcases in a Coles shopping trolley walks into the reserve. He heads for the bench I'm lying on with the backpack as my headrest. I half close my eyes, hoping the stranger will respect my siesta. But I can hear the wheels of the trolley on the concrete path coming closer.

He is a tall man with broad shoulders; he walks with a straight back as he pushes the trolley towards me. Now only a few metres away, I feel just a little uneasy about the tall stranger. I am about to stand up and leave when he greets me with a jovial, 'How're you going?', showing off a decent set of teeth.

My first impression is this man is too well-kept to be homeless. The seam of his navy trousers is neatly ironed, his matching jumper shows no sign of old food or drool. His dark hair is combed backwards; either still damp from a shower or he uses that gel they sell at the barber shop.

As a last attempt to signal I prefer some privacy I don't respond to his greeting. But this man, who I haven't encountered in my two months on the street, introduces himself as 'Travis Dawson, formerly from Maroubra.' I shake his outstretched hand with an unenthusiastic 'David Anderson.' He leaves his trolley on the path and joins me on the bench, close enough for me to notice the absence of body odour.

'Hey, David, can you believe that next month I'll be celebrating my second year away from it all?' The stranger, Travis, makes this announcement with a familiarity as if we've been on his journey together.

'Oh, that's good.'

My lack of interest doesn't stop Travis or 'Trav', as he suggested I call him.

'Mate, I worked my arse off for that outfit. It was my first job after uni, and I went up the ladder like a monkey with a stolen banana.'

I'm not really sure what to say, so I just nod while avoiding eye contact.

'I was the youngest to become a senior manager, just after my thirtieth birthday. I had a corner office with my own secretary.'

This time I feel obliged to offer some acknowledgement.

'Well, Travis, that's impressive at such a young age.'

'I had responsibility for the whole of South Sydney all the way to Port Botany. You can imagine what a heavy load that is to carry in a big telco. I gave them everything and then more without ever asking for a pay rise; that came automatically.'

Travis Dawson now has momentum and only interrupts his journey up the corporate ranks with the occasional snort followed by a deep exhale.

'And then it all turned to shit, mate.'

I wasn't prepared for this sudden twist in his story.

'Really, Travis, what happened?' I hope I have come across as sincere.

'Yeah, the last thing was my job. They walked me out of the office with my career in a cardboard box.'

This man, who I met hardly fifteen minutes ago, now sits with his head bowed. Even if he was bullshitting, maybe just a bit, this is a familiar tale from people I have encountered on the street. Life can be beautiful one day and then someone flicks a switch; like Arthur who didn't make it across the railway crossing.

Travis' story was tough to listen to. He started with pokies at the RSL, had a good run, a holiday in Fiji for the family, private schools for the kids, the big race at Randwick was a certainty but pipped at the post, with VIP status they gave him extended credit at the RSL. He started using the company Amex for personal expenses, his wife Emma's new Lexus was the last fatal mistake. He sold the house to repay his former employer in an agreement that kept him out of jail. Emma and the kids moved in with her parents, Braeden will be seven in December and Sophie starts school next year.

At that moment I decide to believe this stranger, but I don't offer any sympathy.

Behind the wooden fence I hear the little ones starting to leave the childcare centre at the end of their day with calls of 'Goodbye, miss.' The parents will be waiting at the gate on Riley Street.

When I swing the pack onto my back Travis waves with a 'Thank you for listening.'

As a newcomer to this life, I still enjoy the freedom of no particular place to go and no need to glance at my watch. I only need to get back to The Domain before dark.

Soup kitchen on Sussex Street

Word of mouth is how you learn about a decent feed. That's how I discovered the soup kitchen on Sussex Street, at the end of another day of aimless walking.

It is a bitterly cold night with soft but persistent rain, and I am wet through to my underpants. When I sit down with a bowl of spicy tomato soup on the cement veranda, Benny, who I recognise from Arthur's mob outside Central Station, squeezes into a dry spot next to me, within touching distance of the gas heater.

After slurping the last drop of soup from his bowl he wipes his mouth with the sleeve of his pale blue knitted jumper. I offer to take the bowls back inside to the serving table, but Benny says, 'Nah, mate, relax, there will be enough for a second helping.'

I love Benny's brutal honesty. Sitting close to the heater, he does all the talking. I must have shown a hint of disinterest, probably staring past him, because he asks, 'Hey, are you with me or am I boring you?'

Benny doesn't wait for an answer and proceeds to tell me that life on the street started when he was ten years old. It was a whole lot better than at home where his parents hardly acknowledged his existence. 'They were pissed and fighting most of the time.' A sex worker in Kings Cross, much younger than his mother, offered him a blanket and something to eat the night he climbed through his bedroom window. 'That was the first time someone reached out to me without a slap across the face. I just needed to get away to a safe place, I didn't expect such kindness.'

People like Benny are keen to share their life stories. When I watch the tale teller closely, their eyes often look more dead than alive. But there is something different about Benny; his deep brown eyes invite me to make contact, and his eyes smile at me.

I sense it is my turn, my story to tell. I don't talk about my childhood, not a mention of my mother or Trevor Cleary, just the final chapter, struggling at work before I turned my back on my family. Benny's response to my sorry tale is abrupt, as if he could sense my discomfort. 'Mate, you're now with people who understand you.'

I use a second helping of the tomato soup to change the subject.

'Hey, David, look me up when you're in Martin Place,' Benny

calls out as he stands up to leave. I follow shortly afterwards. As I walk under the canopies along King Street for protection against the rain, I reflect on our conversation. I was touched by Benny's story, without blame or regret. I could have asked his surname.

Shelter at Circular Quay

The souls who share life out in the open remind me of statues, I normally find them in the same place. On the city side of Circular Quay, in a sheltered corner, reside Felix and his girlfriend Maria. 'The European connection' as Felix introduced them; Maria's grandparents migrated from Lisbon, but I later found out Felix was born in Sao Paulo in Brazil. They have tried other places across the city, but this concrete and glass corner, close to the Opera House, is Maria's preference. The people coming off the ferries and trains are generous with their tips. There is the late-night handout from the burger joint when they close after the last ferry.

I cross the street from Customs House and notice Maria shifting closer to Felix, to give me a spot on her grey yoga mat. Felix is a tall man; at first his thick eyebrows and prominent jaw under a black beard make him look unfriendly. He says he heard from one of the deckhands on the Manly ferry that we are in for a wet summer with thunderstorms, but Maria dismisses the forecast with a wave of her hand and a long yawn. I notice she has three gold crowns at the back. Life away from home has claimed its scars, but she remains an attractive woman with her long neck and big dark eyes.

Above us an inner-city train screeches, steel on steel, as it pulls up in the station. Then it is quiet until the guard blows the shrill whistle.

'Hey, David, you are a dark horse.' Felix has moved on from the weather forecast.

'Why do you think that, Felix?' I know exactly why; I have enjoyed privacy on the street, I have kept my real-life story out of the conversation.

'We open our hearts; we tell it all. You even know that my father died of a heart attack in a brothel; on the job, so to say. But not our David here; just makes small talk with his posh accent. Boring bullshit talk, I say.'

Next to Maria on the yoga mat, Felix leans forward to make eye contact, as if to show that he is waiting for my answer.

I was fired by the law firm for not turning up at work. That version is at least half of the truth. I always wanted to be a lawyer, but the work was too demanding. But I'm happy now, days turn into weeks, without any commitments and no responsibilities, I've made new acquaintances, some who feel like friends.

Felix doesn't say a word when I wrap up the one-minute summary of my biography. From the corner of my eye, I see him rolling tobacco in a piece of brown paper.

After a long puff he passes the cigarette to Maria and leans forward again.

'Yeh, same old story.'

Before I can say anything, he adds, 'Fancy title but you can't take the heat.'

Felix is right but it doesn't hurt anymore. I have used that same story with other new faces on the street, it keeps my mother and Jennifer and Chloe out of the conversation.

'David, you think we are stupid. Losing your job can't be the only reason you're on the street, mate.'

When I turn my head, I see they are both staring at me.

'Felix, please, let's just leave it there.' I speak softly.

Maria leans over and places her hand with the chipped nail polish on my arm.

The sun has moved behind a high rise, there is a steady stream of people walking quickly to make it to the ferry or the train upstairs. They are heading home after eight hours at work, for some it was probably longer. I think of those still stuck at their desks. A young couple in business suits hold hands as they run past us towards the ferry wharf.

It is time for me to move on. When I stand up Maria says, 'Hey, David, you should look after yourself. You're not alone out here.'

'Thanks, Maria, but I'm doing just fine.'

'Really? Look at yourself. Your sneaker has a hole on the toe, and I don't think you've changed your clothes for weeks.' She leans forward and points at the brown streak on my jeans where I spilled soup a few weeks ago.

'You need a decent wash and clean clothes, David. Promise me, you will go up to the chapel tomorrow. Everyone's welcome there.'

As I swing the pack onto my back Felix says, 'Mate, hope I didn't upset you.'

I nod and say, 'No worries, see you later.'

It is only a short walk up the hill to the tree in the domain. The dome of blue sky promises a comfortable night in the sleeping bag. I am thinking of an early start tomorrow.

Across the Bridge

Arthur is in his regular spot outside Central Station. He has become a close acquaintance; I trust him with my belongings, however meagre, and they all fit into the backpack.

'All good, David, I haven't got any plans for the day,' he says as he takes it from me.

Walking down Elizabeth Street I glance over my shoulder. Arthur is using my pack as a backrest against the wall of the station.

At the highest point on the Anzac Bridge, I stop to drink in the view across the water to the silver office towers with their dark secrets. A ferry looks like a toy boat as it runs towards the Balmain wharf. The last time I made that journey was in my university days for Sunday night dinner with Mum; by then Trevor Cleary had made himself comfortable in my father's chair at the head of the dark wood table.

Walking along the streets of Balmain, even the smell seems familiar. I make my way down a back route away from the busy Darling Street. It is a warm day without a breeze, perspiration trickles into the small of my back. In the park near my old primary school, I find a drinking fountain and then rest for a few minutes on a bench in the shade.

On Duke Street I don't immediately recognise the home where I grew up; the iron-lace balustrade of the upstairs balcony has been replaced with glass panels, the terrace is now painted in steel grey, Mum's favourite sash windows are gone, the street number is embedded into one of the new pillars on either side of the sliding front gate. What was Dad's rose garden has made way for a paved driveway with a black Audi four-wheel drive.

'You are disowned,' was how Mum finished her letter. Most of it would have been dictated by Trevor Cleary, I hardly recognised my mother's voice. The letter was sent to my office address, waiting for me when Jennifer and I returned from our honeymoon. I remember feeling uncomfortable about Mum turning her back on me, but nothing more than that.

Number 7 Duke Street is now home to a family with means. Our working-class taste has been erased by an architect with a different imagination. People like my parents now live a train ride away from the Balmain peninsula. Those who have taken our place are exactly who Mum aspired for us to be.

I heard about Mum's diagnosis when an old neighbour, Mary Livingstone, left a message with my personal assistant. We were in the final stage of a deal, there was a large success fee at stake, and I only called back a few days later. It was a landline number, by the time I spoke to Mary, Mum had passed away at the Concord Hospital, the night before.

A woman in black exercise gear, her brown hair pulled back under a matching cap, closes the front door with a heavy thud and stops on the stairs. She puts on her sunglasses and looks at me across the street, before opening the driver side door of the Audi. I understand her hesitation, an unwashed man in an oversized grey jumper staring at her house on a deserted street. She drives past me slowly, probably wondering whether she should alert the police. I start walking back towards Darling Street, hoping she will see me leaving in her rear-view mirror.

The street doctor

Arthur greets me with 'You're back early' without waiting for an answer. As I collect my backpack, he tells me about a new mobile van with a doctor and a nurse that stops at night in Darlinghurst, apparently down the hill from Oxford Street. Arthur uses his index finger to show me a rotten tooth that keeps him awake at night. I don't tell him about the sharp pain I feel after a meal and that I have been shitting streams of brown foul-smelling liquid, but yes, I'll come along to check out this van with a free doctor.

Just after sunset we spot the white van with a red cross on the side panels. It is parked in a bay reserved for council vehicles, and by the time we walk up there are five people waiting on the footpath. I stay with Arthur in the line, while those ahead of us share their medical conditions. None of it sounds particularly serious, except for a short, thin bloke with a shaven head who has self-diagnosed his condition as a tumour on the brain.

It is Arthur's turn, and he makes his way to the double doors at the back of the van. The doctor, a young man, I estimate in his late twenties with an early bald patch, sits on a stool inside while behind him the nurse is busy unpacking boxes of medicine into a red plastic tray. The doctor invites Arthur to take a seat opposite him on a built-in bench. Arthur opens his mouth wide and explains his tooth problem to the doctor.

I leave Arthur and I wander along Burton Street.

On the next corner is the Darlinghurst Theatre where a spotlight shines on a large poster announcing 'ONCE, the Tony Award winning musical is back!'. I remember this story, originally a movie about a busker who meets a young woman on the streets of Dublin. I would have seen it with Jennifer on one of our movie and dinner nights.

Below the title of the show are the names of the cast. The male actor isn't someone I recognise. On the next line it says, 'And in her debut performance the fabulous Miss Chloe Bradshaw.' Across the street I can see Arthur still in the back of the van with the doctor, but I walk in the opposite direction.

The need to get away from the theatre takes me through Woolloomooloo, past the public carpark and up the hill towards the spotlights shining on Saint Mary's Cathedral. Pushed forward by the desperation to be on my own, I run down the road behind the Sydney Eye Hospital. The weight of the pack on my back doesn't slow me down; I am short of breath, but I keep running to the tree halfway across the dimly lit grass expanse of the Domain.

I roll out my sleeping bag and sit with my back against the rough tree trunk. My hands shake, instinctively I reach into the pockets of my jeans and only find a crumpled-up sheet of toilet paper. I hear the voices of a man and a woman as they walk by; they sound young and cheerful. The nighttime chill creeps under my two layers of clothing. I open the zip and slide down deeper into my sleeping bag. The darkness under the thick summer canopy gradually brings some calm. My breathing has returned to normal, I am tired now, but the sleep doesn't come.

Hopefully Arthur received something for his toothache; the doctor may even have extracted it in the back of the white van. Behind me at the hospital I hear the siren of an approaching ambulance. I have a vivid recollection of the poster in the theatre's window, the white letters on a black background. Chloe Bradshaw, her mother's birth name.

In the eastern sky behind the Art Gallery, I can see lightning. This tree doesn't offer much protection during a thunderstorm, but tonight it seems the storm is moving out to sea.

The chapel in Kings Cross

Nathan, the bloke with the crutch at Central Station, thought it was only one of those bullshit rumours on the street, but when I joined Felix and Maria for a late-night burger last week she invited me personally.

'It would mean a lot to us if you can make it, David, next Wednesday afternoon, three o'clock at the chapel in Kings Cross. I think it will be a little bit formal.'

I remembered Maria's comment about me needing a decent wash. This surprised me at first, I wasn't aware my smell was quite so offensive. But I'd had a hot shower and found a clean navy corduroy shirt and grey pants from Streetlevel up in Surry Hills.

As I make my way from Victoria Street I see a crowd standing outside the chapel. I imagine an odour of soap as I get closer to the gathering of scrubbed-up guests. Arthur is there talking with Benny and a young man in a black tracksuit holding a sausage dog in his arms. When I join them in the shade of the Magnolia tree, I notice a gap where the doctor removed Arthur's tooth.

Travis, the bloke who spoiled my day in Cooper Street Reserve, is surrounded by a group looking uninterested in his animated story. On either side of the entrance to the chapel two tall transvestites in matching pink miniskirts are posing for photographs.

'Here they come,' someone behind me shouts and I see a black London Taxi with its hazard lights flashing. The crowd moves onto the pavement, making room for it to pull up. The back door opens and Maria steps out in a knee length cream-coloured dress. Her dark hair is pulled back in a bun with a band of yellow flowers. She shows off the happiest smile, life on the street is masked with make-up and a full red mouth. Felix follows in a white linen suit, his black beard has been trimmed. He holds out his left arm for Maria, she hooks in, and they walk towards the door where the two transvestites are blowing kisses.

The ceremony lasts no more than 30 minutes before the pastor declares Felix and Maria husband and wife. Felix holds Maria's face in both hands and kisses her, first on the forehead and then a long open mouthed kiss.

A woman in a red and gold kaftan who could be Maria's older sister, also with a dark complexion but not as slender, joins the pastor at the front of the chapel. She smiles at us all and introduces herself as Victoria.

'This is a wonderful moment. There were days, months when I feared for my friend Maria. Some of you may know that we were together in the opera chorus, then for a long time, there was only darkness. Just look at her today; and Felix, the man who came from nowhere.'

Without musical accompaniment, in a haunting soprano voice Victoria sings *O Mio Babbino Caro*. The emotion pushes up in my throat. I swallow and manage not to cry. When Victoria finishes she walks over to Maria and Felix, they embrace in a huddle; and for a few seconds, there is a strange silence inside the chapel.

In the hall next door, we find long trestle tables with white tablecloths, in tall plastic glasses the choice of sparkling wine or orange juice. The wine tastes better than I remember. The guests hover around trays of small hamburgers, and once all the trays are empty, we line up for cups of vanilla ice-cream.

I am about to make a quiet escape when the pastor calls for attention.

'Please allow me one more announcement.' He waits until there is complete silence.

'Today has been very special, for Maria and Felix, our bridal couple, but also their friends, our community of souls who have gathered here to share their joyous day.'

The pastor waits for the applause and whistles to die down.

'It is with gratitude to one of our benefactors that I can announce, from tonight Maria and Felix will sleep with a roof over their heads.' The pastor's announcement is met with a more formal applause, everyone clapping hands but no shouting or whistling.

Next to me Arthur says, 'So that's the way it falls.'

'What do you mean?' I wonder whether I missed something here today.

'There's hope, for some of us.' With that Arthur puts on his Resch's cap before he turns towards the door.

The Darlinghurst Theatre

The trunk of a tall tree gives me a line-of-sight protection from the theatre entrance. After that evening when I first saw her name on the poster, I promised myself to avoid this part of the city. But the risk of reopening a deep wound wasn't enough to keep me away, like a toddler drawn to the temptation of 'Don't touch.'

The poster announces the show time as 8 pm. 'Chloe Bradshaw', I'm not upset that she has taken a new surname. Imagine going through life having to explain that your father, David Anderson, is now a homeless man.

Shortly after 6.30 two men get out of a white sedan car that looks like an Uber; they stand outside the theatre in animated conversation. The shorter one, in an English style flat cap, lights a cigarette with a match.

A rider on a pushbike comes down Burton Street; at the corner the bike mounts the pavement before pulling up near the theatre entrance. The guy with the cap stamps out the cigarette and greets the new arrival with a cheerful, 'Hey, Chloe.' She looks taller than the last time I saw her. She's wearing a dark skirt with boots and a black denim jacket with the collar turned up. Her hair is still blonde, like her mother's, and shortly cropped, almost like a boy. As my daughter locks her bike on to the silver rail near the doorway, I step forward from behind the tree to the edge of the pavement, fighting the urge to run across the street.

The young man who stamped out his cigarette turns and looks in my direction, for a moment the other two follow his gaze. The pool of light from the theatre canopy doesn't reach my side of the street. I turn my back on Chloe, lengthening my stride as I walk away, fighting the urge to run. Around the first street corner I step into the dark cover of a doorway of what looks like a second-hand furniture business. I wait there for a few minutes; I need to be sure nobody followed me. Standing against the cold glass door, I struggle to think clearly. Now that I know it is her and where to find her, do I want to reconnect with my only child? Do I want her to see what her father has become? Or should I just leave her in the life I was so desperate to escape? Am I happy to be alone, out here where I don't need to think about tomorrow?

Without an answer I start walking, towards the city. I haven't eaten today, but it is not hunger that occupies my mind. I have made a decision, at least for now. In the morning, I'll head back to the chapel, not for food or a shower. My head is an empty chamber filled with echoes. I need someone to hold my hand, both my hands with their long dirty fingernails, to pray for me, to help me see another day.

Hyde Park Barracks

During my time as a corporate lawyer, the part of my life I don't think about that often, Martin Place was my playground. There is a five-star hotel, the Intermezzo restaurant and boutiques selling Italian-style suits without price tags. At the top of the hill is the Reserve Bank of Australia. The building stands tall above a settlement of homeless people, who in the morning wash the sleep out of their eyes in the fountain with its silver curtain of sprinkling water.

Benny is one of those permanent residents. I discover that he's a hoarder with more luggage than you could fit onto the back of a Toyota Hilux. He believes that the greater his possessions, or 'balance sheet' as he calls them, the less likely it is that the police will try to move him on from the place he calls home.

I meet up with Benny a couple of days a week, but never during the day on Martin Place. He understands why after I explained that that part of the city is frequented by former colleagues and some of my old clients in power suits. I want to avoid a 'poor old David' moment. They are the ones who will feel most uncomfortable.

At the top of Macquarie Street in the grounds of the Hyde Park Barracks, Benny and I have found a favourite spot for lunch. We meet there when Benny receives salami and cheese rolls, wrapped in silver foil, from the Italian bar opposite where he has set up his shelter.

We sit on a steel bench at a long table attached to the stone wall. From there we can look up at the revolving restaurant on the top floor of Centre Point Tower. There has been the odd day when I wondered, without saying anything to Benny, what it would be like to fly like a bird from up there to the city streets below. I didn't allow this thought to linger.

It's been more than a week since I saw Chloe outside the theatre in Darlinghurst. I decide to tell Benny about the poster with her name, that I went back there a few nights later and waited across the street behind a tree. How badly I wanted to get closer to her but walked away when she looked in my direction.

Benny makes it harder for me by not telling me what to do.

'Do you want to connect with your daughter, David? Is that what you want?'

'I went to the chapel the next day and the pastor prayed for me. After that I was determined to go back to the theatre, that same night.'

'And you didn't. Why not?' Benny screws up his face as if he is in pain and shakes his head.

'I don't think I'm ready.'

'Mate, it shouldn't always be about you.'

I don't respond, Benny stuffs the silver foil into a paper bag and walks to the garbage bin; he shouts over his shoulder, 'So, who do you think is hurting the most?'

Inside the gates on Macquarie Street a group of about twenty people are gathered closely around a tour leader in an orange t-shirt with a small matching flag. They all turn their heads in our direction when Benny's voice echoes across the courtyard.

Outside Nonna's Pies

Another morning of wandering without a destination. I pass the open door of a shop on Cleveland Street. The whiff of freshly baked pastries hits a soft spot in my belly. I don't want to appear as if I am begging, so I move along to the shop window next door. There is no light inside and a sign in red capital letters on the closed door says, 'BUSINESS RELOCATED'. To look busy, I read a smaller notice underneath in child-like handwriting. It explains that 'Southern Electrical' has moved to a new address in Alexandria because of the plans to widen Cleveland Street.

I am about to continue up the street when a voice calls out, 'Hi, there.' She can be described as an ample woman; a white chef's hat sits slightly skew on her dark brown curly hair. She greets me with a wide smile while wiping her hands on a white apron with 'Nonna's Pies' printed on it in a navy-blue arc. People who sell food in this part of the city seem to have an uncanny ability to spot a passer-by in need of something to eat.

The pies are freshly baked on the premises and Nonna offers me the choice of steak and kidney or chicken with mushrooms. When I take a moment to decide, she says I should have both. This is not a dine-in cafe but the woman suggests I take the stool next to the Coke fridge, as she walks behind the counter to the oven.

I start with the steak and kidney and while I am chewing Nonna launches into her first story. Her husband came to Australia from Sicily as a boy, shortly after the last war. That's World War Two, she adds. They met at a dance and their first business was a fruit and vegetable shop in Botany, but Domenico believed that Aussie blokes love pies and that was the way to go. His wife has always been a keen baker and now, forty-one years later, people drive from the Shire for Nonna's Pies.

Domenico died last year, the week after Easter. 'He went quickly and thank the Lord he didn't suffer.' She misses him very much and in his honour she wants to keep the business going.

'I was still wearing black when I received the letter from the council. These people have no regard for a widow in mourning.'

I have taken my second bite into the chicken and mushroom pie. Until now it has been a one-way conversation from behind the pie oven.

'What did the letter say?' I knew the answer after reading the hand-written note next door, but this woman needs someone to talk to right now.

'I don't understand it all, but we need to close for six months. The man, who owns this building with the three shops, says he will be okay because the council offered generous compensation.'

'And then nothing for you as the tenant, after all these years.' Piling shit on those who cannot defend themselves. How many times have I heard these sorry stories.

Nonna, whose first name I haven't asked, is now crying.

'I'm sorry, but I still get upset every time I talk about this.' She takes a paper napkin from the counter to blow her nose.

'You have been very kind, thank you for the pies. They were delicious.' With that I walk out without looking over my shoulder.

On Cleveland Street it is lively with pedestrians, some step aside when they see me coming. My early morning hunger is gone but my mind is occupied by the woman who is about to lose her life's work. The last few weeks have not been easy. My self-centred existence has been disturbed, seeing Chloe outside the theatre and now this morning, the injustice facing the generous woman at the pie shop. I am unsettled by these developments. More than that, I am frustrated right now, even a little pissed-off. It just seems unfair that these burdens follow me everywhere in life.

An Australia Post vehicle slams its breaks and stops within touching distance. The driver, an Indian man with a purple turban, calls me an idiot. I apologise and step back to the safety of the pavement. It was a close call; it was my fault.

For the rest of the morning, I walk aimlessly, one city block after another. I wrestle with these new questions being asked of me. I rewind to the image of the girl, a woman now, outside the theatre. The laugh that I'd recognise anywhere. Should I cross that street next time? My thoughts drift to the sobbing widow at the pie shop. I can help this woman, should I go back tomorrow?

The sky turns darker early afternoon, the first shower drifts across the city by the time I make it back to the road leading to the Gallery. The clouds look heavy. Tonight I'll need better protection than the tree in the Domain. I am early enough to secure a private corner in the entrance to the carpark. By nightfall I share the corner with Travis the gambler and two other familiar faces whose names I don't know. One of them, a young woman probably still in her twenties with bright red lipstick, has her arm in a sling. I recognise her from the line at the street doctor. I am not used to sharing bedtime with anyone else. I pull up the hood of my jacket, but I can still hear Travis snoring. At times it sounds as if he is being throttled. The woman with the broken arm moans softly in her sleep.

I am awake at dawn. I sit up in my sleeping bag, my mouth is dry, my tongue stuck to my palate. The rain has stopped and there is the promise of a sunny morning. When sleeping rough the early light often brings fresh hope, just the possibility that the loneliness, sometimes despair, may ease off as the day reveals itself. I leave the others still fast asleep and make my way up the hill to the toilet at St James Station.

Back on Cleveland Street

I shall explain to Nonna that I am a qualified lawyer, even though that may be hard for her to believe. I'll ask if I can please see the letter from the council, the notice that demands that her shop be vacated by the end of the year. This is what I am trained for. I will find a flaw in the landlord's ruthless excuse for not offering compensation; she deserves to continue her family business. Once I've read the eviction notice I shall draft a letter on her behalf, it should be clear that she understands her legal rights. It would have helped if I could sign as her lawyer, but that is not possible now.

I arrive outside Nonna's Pies early, there's already a line of customers out the door. Rather than hanging around I walk back to Elizabeth Street, I'll return to offer my help later in the morning. The last time I had something to eat was the two pies yesterday at Nonna's, so I walk to the Salvation Army kitchen on Albion Street where they offer a hot meal on Wednesday mornings.

Most food is edible when you are really hungry, another of life's lessons out here, but this morning the thick vegetable soup with a wholemeal bread roll is even better than I remember from the previous visit. A woman, probably my age, with grey hair below her shoulders and wearing a long floral skirt and red thongs, takes the plastic chair next to me. Her heels are rough and cracked, but her toenails are perfectly painted bright red. She offers me half of her bread roll which I use to wipe the last of my soup from the plastic bowl.

She is not from around here, her name is Mary-Ann, she moved to Sydney from Nowra where she worked as a waitress, but she was also a singer in a band. Her parents may still be alive, but she is not sure. She remembers her father's temper, his large rough hands, her mother held her own and bought a gun from a farmer.

'Mary-Ann is not my real name,' she says with a serious face and finds the butt of a cigarette in the pocket of her khaki shirt. I don't ask her real name, instead I compliment the soup and tell her about the kind woman at the pie shop. Thank you, but she is a vegetarian, hasn't always been but she feels it is just healthier, cauliflower is her favourite veggie.

I head back towards Nonna's, but by the time I reach Elizabeth Street where I should turn left, I have changed my mind. That woman needs help, but I'd rather not get involved. I hover outside the front window of Graphic Man; they offer 'walk–in tattoos with a complimentary cappuccino'.

Four bullets

'What were they thinking?' Benny has this habit of launching into a new rant without what I would call a preamble. We are sharing a bench in Hyde Park, near the Anzac Memorial. I have no idea what comes next, so I keep quiet.

Benny points to the sculpture to our left; four upright bullets with silver points and three shells lying on the ground. I am about to respond with a 'So what?' but then I get it. He is objecting to the symbol of bullets within a short distance of the memorial with its sculpture of three women carrying the body of a fallen soldier. I have followed Benny inside the memorial on several occasions, standing a respectful distance away as he removed his cap.

I acknowledge his annoyance with an abrupt, 'Stupid.'

'Exactly, mate.'

I enjoy his company without having to make conversation.

Benny takes his silver harmonica from an inside pocket of his worn leather waistcoat. I remain quiet as he warms up his lips with a loud sucking sound, before he plays a slow rendition of 'Blowin' in the Wind'. It strikes me that Benny seldom plays happy tunes. He prefers songs that protest about loss or injustice. I wonder whether he is even aware of this. He's bloody good on the harmonica, and I lean back to enjoy the music, feeling a little mellow in the midday sun.

Benny interrupts my slumber, as he shakes the spit out of it.

'Hey, David, can you play an instrument?'

'Not really.'

'Shit, mate, what sort of an answer is that? You can either play something or you can't.'

'I took piano lessons when I was in primary school, but I ended up in the boys' choir.'

'Hmm, a singer then. Come on, let's do something together.'

'No, Benny, it's been a long time.'

'Okay, you call the song. Something you remember from school.'

It's obvious that he won't let me get away without a song. While I'm still struggling with a suggestion Benny starts to play and I recognise the tune of 'The Tenterfield Saddler'.

I cough to clear my throat and keeping my voice down, I join in after the first chorus. As we get further into the song I'm a little more relaxed but still sing softly, conscious of people walking past us.

When we wrap up the closing lyrics, Benny shakes his head and says, 'Not bad, mate.' He starts to play another song that I don't recognise, then stops abruptly and puts the harmonica into the pocket of his waistcoat.

'David, I've been thinking, it is not safe for you to be on your own at night.'

I didn't expect this sudden change of mood, so I say, 'Really?'

'Yeah, mate. A bloke I've talked to a few times at the late-night food truck near Saint Vinnies was badly beaten up. He's in a coma now, they don't think he's going to make it.'

Benny's information is normally reliable; I know he keeps up with the news. On Martin Place, at the end of the day, he gets a copy of the *Telegraph* from the guy at the newspaper and fruit stall. Benny thinks this bloke may be Russian, so he's given him the nickname Igor.

The man slept under a tree in Moore Park, he was a loner. Benny's news about someone I've never met upsets me. I am in my third year of freedom; my belongings have always fitted into the backpack I bought for the family hiking holiday in the Snowy Mountains. The sleeping bag, a handout from the chapel, fits neatly into the top of the backpack. It allows me to move around the city with everything I own.

When I stopped outside a shop window on Castlereagh Street yesterday, I realised my hair could do with a generous dollop of shampoo; my beard has grown into my nostrils, and you can hardly see my teeth when I put on a smile. I have lost weight; I slouch but I still imagine a sparkle in my eye. I'm aware that my easy-going demeanour can be misleading. I become frustrated when some shit interrupts my life on the city streets; like this man with tubes up his nostrils, waiting to die.

On Benny's insistence I join him after sunset at the top of Martin Place. I only need space for my backpack and sleeping bag, but on arrival my new roommate suggests that I make my bed on two wooden pallets he has handy in case of a visitor.

'This way you stay off the ground on a rainy night.'

Benny understands me; he is not an intruder into my private thoughts. We spend our first night together with little conversation. I lie in my sleeping bag listening to his harmonica; I recognise a few of the songs and sing along softly, just to myself.

✦

Martin Place has gone quiet, we've finished the last of the bread rolls from the bakery on Pitt Street. Benny's mate Igor, the Russian, has passed on four brown bananas and a half-bottle of peach brandy. I bring the bottle to my mouth without swallowing. Benny sniggers when I hand it back.

With the hood of my ski jacket over my head, I turn away from the streetlamp. I am vaguely aware of the traffic on Macquarie Street as I drift into sleep. I dream of an angry scream; it's Benny's voice. There's water dripping on my sleeping bag. The weather must have turned.

'Let me go, you filthy bastard.' This time it is not Benny. I am awake now.

In the pool of light from the streetlamp, I see two bodies wrestling on the ground. I recognise Benny, the other is in a business suit. There is another guy in a suit with his tie undone; he walks in a circle around Benny and the man he is fighting.

'Jesus Christ, he has a knife.' I can hear the terror in his voice as he starts kicking at Benny, who seems to have the upper hand in the tussle on the ground. By the time I escape my sodden sleeping bag the second guy has grabbed Benny's ponytail and is trying to pull him off his friend, who's pinned to the ground.

'Let go, you piece of shit, or I'll cut his throat.'

I now see the silver blade in Benny's hand. The young man

lets go of Benny's hair and runs towards Martin Place Station.

I go down on my knees and ask Benny to please put the knife away. It is too late; there's blood on the white shirt collar of the man on the ground. He is crying, begging, 'Please don't hurt me.'

But Benny holds the blade against his throat.

Two police cars with their lights flashing pull up on Macquarie Street. I stand up but Benny doesn't move; he has a knee on the young man's back, with his left hand pulling his hair backwards and the knife still in his right fist.

With two policemen standing over him, their black revolvers drawn, Benny stands up slowly and drops his knife on the ground. The policeman closest to him kicks it away, with his revolver aimed at Benny's chest. I see the second suit, who ran to the station, walking back up the steps.

The young man with blood on his collar stands up and presses a white tissue against the cut on his throat. He can only be in his mid-twenties, athletically built with a dark curl on his forehead. We are on our knees; a policeman forces my arms behind my back and then the cold steel of the handcuffs.

'Gentlemen, what happened here tonight?' I am not sure whether the policeman means all four of us.

The guys in suits look at each other without saying a word.

I am surprised by the calmness in Benny's voice as he, still on his knees next to me, tells the policemen that the two of us had an early night, probably asleep by ten but he doesn't carry a watch. He woke up and his first thought was that it had started raining. When he moved the cardboard boxes off his body, he saw these two guys standing next to where we slept. 'Cock in hand and giggling while spraying the piss over me and my mate David.'

The second policeman asks the two men to follow him, and they engage in whispered conversation away from where Benny and I are kneeling on the concrete steps. This carries on for at least ten minutes before the officer returns and we are marched to the police cars, their lights again flashing blue and red.

Surry Hills Police Station

Benny and I are separated while the police take our statements. Then, with our handcuffs removed, two officers in uniform march us to the door at the end of the corridor. Our cell has two beds, each with a pillow and a grey blanket. When Benny asks whether we can have a shower to wash the piss off our bodies, the policeman just laughs and asks whether we think we have booked into a hotel.

We lie in silence. It seems a quiet night for the local police, except I think I recognise the voices of the two young men from Martin Place in the charge office. Unbeknown to Benny and me as we stretch out on our beds, their version of what happened earlier tonight differs substantially from what we told the police.

Yes, they had a leak after a few beers at a pub on George Street, but it was a good five metres away from where the 'two hobos' were sleeping. Then one of them jumped up, pulled a knife and knocked him over. 'He was on my back with the knife against my throat. My friend tried to help me, that's when the second hobo charged and knocked him to the ground.' The first man tells the police he didn't offer any resistance. Says he could feel the cold blade of the knife against his throat and blood trickle down his neck. 'I really thought he was going to cut my throat.'

After a while I only hear the duty officers talking among themselves, and the occasional laugh. I close my eyes, hoping that sleep will come. This is the first night I have spent indoors since leaving the apartment in Rushcutters Bay. I hear Benny's voice; he is repeating my name. When I open my eyes he is sitting at the foot of my bed.

'David, I think I am in trouble.'

In a whispered tone Benny tells me about a previous conviction. He was only a young man working for a furniture removal company in Campbelltown. It was outside a pub, over Easter weekend; he didn't start the fight, but he couldn't stop hitting, even after his attacker was unconscious. Benny knows I am a lawyer, or rather was a lawyer. It is a reasonable expectation that I can help him.

'That may become an issue, Benny, but I think we should just deal with what happened tonight. Let's wait until we know what those young blokes told the police.'

I need to offer Benny some reassurance, some hope that there may not be a second charge against him.

'Shit, mate, I had a knife in my hand. I should've got rid of it when I heard the cop cars coming.'

'I know. Seeing you with a knife against the man's throat

could reflect badly on us, but the police won't ignore our defence. Our stories are the same; two people fast asleep being pissed on by drunk, self-entitled idiots.'

'David, I don't want you to get into trouble here. I'm the one who loses my temper without thinking.'

'Benny, we're in this together. Let me handle the talking from now on.'

He looks at me before he wipes his hand across his face; when he leans forward he is close enough for me to smell the peach brandy.

'Thank you, mate. This is the first time someone has shown up for me, ever.'

I put my hand on his bare forearm and suggest we should try to get some rest.

Staring at the raw concrete ceiling, I can hear Benny's rhythmic snoring. I retrace a long walk that started in the kitchen of our Woollahra home, the first night under the stars on the Domain, sleeping in the doorways of unknown addresses. Tonight I enjoy the comfort of a mattress with my head on a pillow, but behind the steel bars of a police cell. Since walking away from my family, escaping my career responsibility, I have shared my life with warm hearts, like Benny Mansfield, my roommate. On the street we have a common need for connection. We laugh at the corniest of jokes; we live in a place where people really want to know how you are. Everyone has a story to tell, the honesty comes without an alibi. I am surrounded by a community that holds my story. Then, watching Chloe arrive outside the theatre was an unsettling experience. I couldn't embarrass her, not in the company of friends, my unwashed body and dirty clothes. She would have smelled my life on the street, this man who once was her father.

I must have fallen asleep, properly, because the flushing of the toilet wakes me and I sit up. Benny pulls up the zip of his jeans as he walks back to his bed. The pale-yellow light stayed on all night, but through a small window high on the wall above me I can see the greyness of the morning.

Benny and I remain on our beds, as if we want to make the most of this privilege, until I hear the rattling of keys. The policeman who walks in is a short, stocky bloke with a dark moustache, not one of the team who brought us in the night before. I expect a slice of bread, perhaps even a mug of coffee, but the copper comes empty handed.

Without putting us back in handcuffs he barks, 'Follow me.'

The sergeant behind a desk with a stack of brown folders tells Benny and me that we're free to go. He appears a little disappointed as he explains there was a third guy in Martin Place who ran away when Benny pulled the knife. He came to the station later last night to make a statement.

'This little prick told a different story to his mates. He confessed they pissed on you, on their way home from the pub. Claims it wasn't his idea. They don't want to lay a charge, probably worried it will get into the newspaper, worried about their jobs in the fancy part of town.'

The sergeant laughs when Benny asks whether they will give us a lift 'back home' to Martin Place. 'On your way, mate, and hey, you're not getting that knife back.' With that he uses his thumb to show us the front door onto Goulburn Street.

Still smelling of piss we walk towards Museum Station. I hope the young couple at the take-away cart will offer us each a long black. Benny leads the way, and I notice that in spite of his awkward stride because of his bandy legs, he walks with purpose; shoulders pulled back and his spine as straight as an iron rod.

While we wait for the light to change at the busy Liverpool Street crossing, he starts laughing. 'I bet this is the last time those boys'll piss on a bloke sleeping rough.'

Clarence Street

I am one of the last diners, so to say, to leave the soup kitchen. Benny left earlier, complaining about a long day on his feet. The night air is cool with winter approaching when I make my way up the hill towards Wynyard Station. I figure out the shortest route back to Benny's shelter is along Clarence Street, where the traffic going to the Harbour Bridge is still heavy. Walking on the right-hand side of the street, I hear loud voices and laughter, but I don't see any pedestrians until it is too late. Two men in dark suits are followed closely by two women sharing a joke as they walk up the stairs from the restaurant. I realise I am trapped outside the entrance to the Sydney institution known for its power tables.

The man closest to me is Alexander Fox, one of my former partners. His eyes grow larger as he stares at me. I feel the urge to run across three lanes of traffic. The women have gone quiet, as if they are waiting for Alexander to say something or do something, about this filthy man blocking their way.

'David Anderson, is that you?'

'Good evening, Alexander,' I say softly.

It has been close to three years since my last day in the office. After the partners' meeting, where I would have been dismissed in absentia, there was probably just an all-staff memo: 'David Anderson has left the firm, for personal reasons.'

I haven't showered for days and I am suddenly aware of my smell, an odour that can hang around like a rubbish bin. I consider offering a handshake, but instead I put my right hand in the pocket of my track pants. I am conscious of the searching eyes of Alexander's three companions who have moved towards their car where the driver waits with both doors open.

'Do you live around here?' Alexander asks and makes a circular movement with the index finger of his left hand. I cannot help noticing his initials embroidered on the double cuff of his white shirt.

'Not far from here,' I say and point to no particular place.

'Alex, it's getting late.' It must be his wife calling from the car.

'David, I better get going. What a surprise.'

'Yes, good to see you, Alexander.'

I stand outside the entrance to the restaurant and watch as the black car pulls slowly into the traffic on Clarence Street.

Relocation to East Sydney

Benny says he received a message the pastor wanted to see him and suggests we walk up to Kings Cross. At the chapel, the pastor asks Benny to come to his office for a chat. I wait on a bench in the front garden, and when he joins me outside, he smiles without trying to hide his missing teeth.

The pastor has offered him a roof over his head. 'It's only small and just up the road from Martin Place, in East Sydney.' I'm happy for him, but I'll miss his closeness, the hours together just staring at nothing, the meals we share, however meagre, the bedtime melodies on his harmonica. In Benny I have found a man who senses my vulnerability.

After he 'relocates' as he calls it, I move closer to Central Station. This feels like a part of the city with heart; the shop owners are generous with their food, there is good protection in doorways after dark. On this night I wander away from the station, still deciding where to sleep. At a two-storey terrace a stream of light comes through a gap in the curtains. Inside I can see a woman brushing her long black hair. She's wearing white underwear. I stop to look at her, before walking, fast, across the street. I settle for a spot partly under cover outside the roller door of 'THE TAX MAN'. The image of the woman stays with me. It has been a very long time since I have felt any affection, even just a hand against my cheek. A shiver makes me pull up the zipper of my sleeping bag.

Early the next morning I discover that the roller door leads to off-street parking for the owner's black Mercedes sports car. With the sunglasses and grey felt hat he looks more like a gangster in a Hollywood film. He waits while I roll up my sleeping bag before squeezing his car into the narrow space; I thank him for his patience. When he takes a ten dollar note out of his wallet I say, 'No, thank you, I don't need any money.' Instead I ask whether he would be kind enough to share a few blank pages of paper and a pen.

I rest the sheets of paper on my backpack and start writing a letter, one meticulous sentence at a time, careful with my spelling. I am comfortable with the logic, but the legal considerations present more of a challenge. Is it possible that I erased a law degree and almost twenty years in practice in return for this life of empty days? I persevere and below 'sincerely' on the second page I leave room for a name, signature and address. After a final spell check I walk back inside and return the pen to where the owner sits behind his desk. I fold the pages in half before walking down the hill to Nonna's Pies.

Nonna is happy to see me and invites me in for a pie and coffee, but I explain that I just want her to read the letter, which I place on the glass counter. When Nonna asks me to wait while she gets her glasses that are in the back of the shop, I walk out and keep going in the direction of East Sydney, hoping to see Benny around.

Elizabeth near Belvoir

The 'grand opening' of Nonna's Pies on Elizabeth Street near the Belvoir Street intersection is a modest affair. She insisted that I invite Benny to join her family for pies fresh out of the oven, with cappuccinos from the new machine imported by her son-in-law Mario.

The new shop has room for a long communal table, and there are seven of us around it on straight back chairs, including Nonna's two daughters Francesca, wife of Mario, and her younger sister Sofia. Also invited is a regular customer Raymond, a burly carpenter from Rockdale who built the shelves and counter.

After a second round of coffees Nonna stands up at the head of the table. Between the tears and blowing her nose in a paper napkin, she recalls the dark days when she faced eviction back on Cleveland Street. Her hard earned reputation as a baker of pies, made possible by the generosity of her husband Domenico, who is looking down on us today, was about to be taken away from her.

Mario, a handsome Italian man with dark slicked-back hair and a wine-red bowtie, stands up and puts his arm around her.

'Then this man, this wonderful clever man came into my shop.' Nonna sniffs and holds out her hand with an open palm to where I am sitting at the opposite end of the table.

'The letter you wrote for the *Telegraph*, that changed everything.'

Next to me Benny stands and starts clapping, and the others join in the applause.

'Forgive my English, but after that letter the whole of Sydney knew I was being screwed by my landlord,' Nonna continues.

With his arm resting on her shoulder, Mario responds with a deep belly laugh.

'David, God bless you, my child,' Nonna says.

When she sits down, still wiping her tears, Benny is on his feet.

'In a few months from now I'll turn fifty and that means it'll be close to forty years since I first found myself on the street.' He pauses, almost as if he is waiting for a response from the group around the table.

'Forty years without family or anybody I could call a friend. That was until I met my mate David over here.' He nods in my direction.

'You can be full of shit sometimes, David Anderson, but I love you, mate.'

I shift in my chair, but Benny hasn't finished yet.

'Nonna, you give David credit for the letter that helped with the payout and now this new shop, which I must say, is not too shabby.' Then that tight lipped smile. 'What you have given back is more than a few warm pies.' Benny pauses and I think he is quite a confident speech maker.

'Out there we float like autumn leaves in the breeze, until we come crashing down. Nonna, now that David helps you in the shop, you have given him something to hold onto.'

Then Benny is done, and he sits down.

Nonna allows tears and snot to mix as she makes her way around the table and embraces me. I stand up to start clearing the empty cups and paper plates.

Benny grabs my arm and says he's inviting a few friends over to his place for tea and donuts; he winks and says there may be something stronger afterwards. 'Wednesday afternoon

When Only Today Matters

next week and no later than three o'clock,' he warns me with
his arthritis bent index finger.

Benny's place on Francis Street

After a shower at the chapel and receiving a clean shirt and
underpants from the volunteers there, I walk down William
Street, excited about sharing Benny's pride in his own place.
I expect there will be other familiar faces; maybe Igor from
Martin Place, and Suzanne who Benny introduced to me one
evening back at the soup kitchen as 'an old girlfriend'.

His is one of four apartments in a brown face brick building.
The door on the street is open and I make my way up the stairs
to number 3. I need to tread carefully because there is little
light in the stairwell except for the window on the landing.

On the first floor there are two doors, and I can see a small
number 3 in silver on the door to my right. From behind the
door of the second apartment I can hear Jim Maxwell's voice on
the radio. Jim says the score is two for 94 in the thirtieth over.
I didn't know Australia was playing a cricket series at home.

I knock on the door of number 3 and hear brisk footsteps.
Benny must have been waiting for the first guest to arrive.

'Good to see you, mate.' He gestures for me to come in.

There is a small couch with a black and beige check blanket
draped over it. Against the wall Benny has stacked all his
belongings from Martin Place, even the wooden pallets, milk
crates and the pile of flattened cardboard boxes. I hear the click
of the door closing behind me.

Chloe stands up from a chair near the kitchen bench. I hesitate, not sure what to do or what to say. I glance over my shoulder; Benny is there, looking me in the eye. My daughter walks slowly, the four steps that separate us. She reaches out and takes my hand. Her fingers are soft but strong. At that moment I am grateful for the shower and clean clothes from the chapel. She pushes the fingers of her other hand through my uncombed bush of curls. I pull her face into my shoulder.

Benny has moved to the kitchen sink where he fills the kettle with water. Chloe and I remain standing, we haven't said a word. My heart is pounding.

Benny breaks the silence with, 'Okay, time for a cuppa.'

He offers no apology for lying about the tea party, but waves towards the couch for Chloe and me to sit down.

I hold her hand as Chloe tells me about the evening when Benny waited for her outside the theatre. She'd walked away from this man she had never seen before, but then Benny said, 'Chloe, I want to talk to you about your father.'

The next morning they met at a cafe on Stanley Street. The disguise of a tea party was Benny's idea. Chloe would arrive early with a bag of fresh donuts. Benny was adamant I wouldn't turn up if I knew about their plan.

The streetlights are on by the time we leave, Chloe's pushbike is chained to a lamppost on the opposite side of Francis Street. One last wave before she rides down the hill and into Stanley Street.

I swing the pack over my shoulder and start walking into the mild spring evening.

Usually by this hour I will have found a sheltered spot to roll out my sleeping bag. But tonight there's an urge to keep moving. After dark, pedestrians step off the footpath when they see a man with a wild beard carrying a backpack; some look nervous and cross the street. Dogs bark at my shadow, at street corners I change direction without reason or purpose. I lose track of whether I am in Surry Hills or Redfern or is this Waterloo already?

Step by step I replay the afternoon in Benny's apartment.

Chloe graduated from the performing arts school. She had a few minor roles in film and TV commercials, then the break in *Once*. I hope I said I was proud of her. She's in a steady relationship and they live in her apartment in Kings Cross. With the money I transferred into her name she didn't need a mortgage. She'd discovered the money when a statement arrived from the bank, weeks after I left home.

I remained silent as Chloe, without invitation, started talking about Jennifer. Her mother could never forgive me for letting her down; she has a new partner, a surgeon who was a school friend of her older brother, there is a vineyard in the Hunter Valley. I felt no envy, no anger. I have allowed my memory of our relationship to fade away, like a childhood fable. Chloe asked if I wanted to see a recent photograph, on her phone, I shook my head.

'Do you mind if we talk more about you, Chloe?'

I dragged out her years since I left home, the milestones I missed, with questions and more questions, hoping to delay sharing details of my life on the street.

But Chloe was persistent; she wanted to know where I get my food, I've lost so much weight, where do I sleep, the clothes I am wearing, where do they come from, what do I do when I'm not well, when I need a doctor, do I have anybody other than Benny who looks out for me, that night outside the theatre, why didn't I just cross the street?

Her last words as we were leaving Benny's apartments were, 'Dad, I won't allow you to disappear again.' I sensed her frustration, perhaps anger, as she grabbed the front of my shirt.

The neighbour downstairs

Chloe paid the deposit and six months' rent for number 2 on the ground floor in the same building as Benny's apartment.

On the day I receive the key Chloe and her partner Erica arrive in a rented van. When we start offloading there is a single bed, a small wooden table with two matching chairs and a well-worn Persian rug. While Chloe and I carry the furniture into the apartment Erica goes over to the van and returns with two large Target bags, holding a couple of bath towels, a doona, a set of bed sheets and a pillow. For my little kitchen there is two of everything, plates, mugs, glasses, cutlery and a bread tin.

Benny comes downstairs and shouts, 'Welcome, neighbour' through the open door. I invite him in, but he says it is a perfect day for fresh air and he is thinking of a stroll down to the Botanical Gardens.

When Erica leaves for work, Chloe follows me into the apartment and locks the door. She pours two glasses of water from the tap over the kitchen sink and hands me one but remains standing.

'Dad, what really happened to you? I still don't understand why you've ended up living on the street. Was this sacrifice really worth it? Or even necessary?'

I am not able to look her in the eye and I wipe the ring of water from the bottom of my glass. No one has asked me this question so directly.

'I have always been anxious, Chloe, from a young age.'

'Anxious about what, Dad?' she demands as she sits at the table.

'About not being good enough, I guess.' I am surprised by my ready admission.

'Mum didn't tell me you have issues with anxiety. All I knew was that you walked away from your job, your life, from both of us.'

'It was a long time coming, in the end I just needed to get away.'

My explanation feels weak as it hangs in the air of the sparsely furnished room. Chloe has her eyes fixed on me.

'Surely you could have taken medication. Did you ever try to get help?'

'I did, Chloe. I started with the occasional tablet before a meeting, eventually I couldn't function without the medication, and other drugs. It got out of hand.'

She shakes her head, before she slowly releases a deep sigh.

'And now, where do you get the money for the medicine? And to support your habit?'

'There are days when I struggle, but I manage without any drugs; an unforeseen blessing for turning my back, for walking away.'

My daughter stares at me, as if she is trying to decide whether that is the truth.

'And you and Mum, wasn't there any way you guys could work things out?' This is the question I'd anticipated from the moment she locked the door.

'She felt the shame too strongly. This isn't a nice thing to say about your mother, but my success as a lawyer was part of the package in our marriage. I knew that from the beginning.'

Chloe's response is an uncomfortable silence, she bites her bottom lip.

'I'm sorry if this comes across as an interrogation, but what about your career. Surely you miss the stimulation, the legal challenges, always a new horizon?'

'Chloe, out here only today matters. That's all I can handle right now.'

'But you were so successful, Dad, your photo on the front page of the newspaper when you won that award, the big salary.'

'I've lowered my expectations.'

I hope my abrupt answers come across as honest. Chloe shakes her head, with a wrinkled frown between her eyes.

'Something else, Dad. I can't remember you ever talking about your family, apart from losing your dad when you were young.'

I stare at my daughter, her dark eyes waiting for a response.

'This seems pathetic now, but I was embarrassed about my family. We were not of the same standing as the Bradshaws.'

Chloe stands up to refill her glass without offering me more water.

'That's a shocking thing to say. Your mother, my grandmother, would have been a widow, a single parent. How can that be embarrassing?'

My daughter doesn't hide her frustration.

'After I lost my father there was another man, in our house. I struggled with that; the truth is I turned my back on my mother.'

'What the hell! Was that fair?'

'At the time I was angry, but she didn't deserve that.'

Chloe sits down on the chair opposite me. I hope she'll talk about something else.

'Can you tell me more about my grandmother?' She leans forward with her elbows resting on the table.

'I owe my life to your grandmother, although it may not seem like much now.'

'Yeah, but what was she like, as a person?' Chloe demands.

'Unselfish and kind, her dream was for me to progress beyond our neighbourhood. It became a bit of an obsession with her.'

Like an accomplished card player, Chloe doesn't respond immediately.

'So, you blame her for the fact that you couldn't hold on to your job, the way you just walked away from your family, all that.'

When I speak it is like a stream of vomit.

'I was the one motivated by that next step on the ladder, it always seemed within reach, my mother made the sacrifices but I was the one who craved recognition and praise, I was so determined not to look over my shoulder that I forgot where I came from, I stepped over bodies in my quest for personal accolades, one of those was my mother, I looked the other way at a time she needed me, when it was my turn to show just a little bit of compassion. Then when the tide turned against me, when I couldn't face up to the next challenge, when I felt alone and scared, she was no longer there to hold my hand. I wasted it all, eventually my own family, you, Chloe.'

My confession hung in the air between us.

There is a knock on the door and Benny calls my name, but Chloe and I remain silent. He doesn't knock again, and I can hear his footsteps going up the stairs.

'This may seem a strange question, but what did my grandmother look like?'

'Like you, Chloe, with the short blonde hair and your dark eyes. There is a very strong resemblance; perhaps more so than with your own mother.' I didn't keep a photograph of my mother; my daughter has never seen an image of her grandmother.

Chloe leans back in her chair; I can see her swallow. This is painful but I'm relieved we can open these festering wounds.

'I probably know the answer, Chloe, but what made you change your surname?'

She hesitates and looks me in the eye.

'Grandpa told me to do it. He said an Anderson doesn't

exist in his life.' My only child looks away to the sash window and wipes her nose with the back of her hand.

'Chloe, I am so sorry. I hope you can forgive me for just walking away.'

'You were brave, Dad. I didn't know that at the time.' Chloe speaks with a woman's voice, no longer a girl.

We sit in silence until she says it is time for her to leave. I walk behind my daughter. When she reaches the door and turns I wrap my arms around her. Chloe grabs my elbow in a firm grip. The door closes and I'm on my own. Suddenly I am exhausted, not like a fourteen-hour day on Level 42, rather a happy tired. I lie down on the bare mattress without taking off my sneakers.

Opening night

I wait outside the theatre where small lights flash on and off around the bright red neon sign announcing, *Merrily We Roll Along*. Through the open doors I can hear a bell ring, followed by an announcement that tonight's performance will commence in five minutes. In my hand are the two tickets Chloe dropped off at the apartment earlier today.

It is unlike Benny to be late. He was very excited when Chloe told us about her role in the new production. I know he had an afternoon shift at the garden centre where he waters the plants for cash in hand, but we had arranged to meet here no later than twenty to eight.

On the further call 'All patrons please take your seats' I see

Benny inside the glass doors waving to attract my attention. We make it to our seats in the second row just as the lights go down, then the sound of a piano fills the theatre.

An older woman called Mary walks on to the stage. I glance over at Benny and his frown suggests he may be equally confused. Then this woman breaks into song, and I recognise my Chloe. Benny pushes his elbow into my rib cage. After a few more songs I figure out that the musical starts with the main characters at an older age; from there it moves backwards to their youth. Now I can sit back and relax.

Benny leans over and whispers, 'Mate, what a wonderful voice.'

In the final act Chloe is the person I know, with her natural blonde hair. She walks with that familiar bounce before she meets up with her two friends, both male characters. When the cast returns for the second encore Benny and I stand up to applaud; the entire theatre rises for a standing ovation. There are shrill whistles and bravos from a group of young people in the row behind us.

Chloe mentioned drinks with the cast afterwards and Benny is keen to stay. I excuse myself to go to the toilet. Downstairs I keep walking, through the double sliding doors and away from the theatre. I only slow down once I turn the corner into Crown Street. At this hour there aren't many pedestrians in this part of the city, I wander back to the apartment, my heart filled with the joy of Chloe's voice.

Lying on my bed fully dressed, with my shoes on the floor, I wait for Benny's footsteps in the stairwell. After a while my eyes grow heavy, I'm thinking Benny must be enjoying himself with the cast. I just hope he takes it easy with the drinks. My plan is to buy a card from the newsagent tomorrow morning and leave it for Chloe at the theatre in a sealed envelope, with a bunch of flowers. I want to say more than congratulations.

Afternoon in Matraville

Nonna suggested I borrow a jacket from her son-in-law Mario. The arms of the navy blazer are a bit long, but with my clean pair of jeans and a white shirt I feel respectable as I wait outside the apartment. It is shortly after two o'clock when I see Chloe's silver two-door Toyota come up the hill from Stanley Street. I wait for her to turn the car around before opening the door on the passenger side.

She only passed her test recently and isn't a confident driver. It is an automatic, and she holds the steering wheel with both hands as she leans forward in the driver's seat. I thank her for the lift and then there is a welcome silence as she concentrates on making her way through the traffic. We merge onto the highway towards the airport and Chloe leans back. She exhales slowly as if she has just climbed a set of stairs.

'I still can't believe this has happened. He was full of fun the night after the show. My friends in the cast all talked about him the next day. What a character; his comments on our performances, the way he smiled, determined not to show his missing teeth.'

Four days ago, I was helping Nonna on the early afternoon

shift when two policemen walked into the pie shop. When I asked what pie they would like the older man with stripes on the sleeve of his uniform introduced himself as Sergeant Carter. I nodded when he asked whether I was David Anderson.

The two officers and I sat down at the communal table and Nonna brought over a bottle of tap water with three glasses. The sergeant did all the talking while the other guy had a notebook and yellow BIC pen in front of him on the table. I felt the scrutiny of his darting eyes behind the dark framed glasses.

Sergeant Carter said he believed I knew Benny Mansfield. I told him I am a friend of Benny's, our apartments are in the same building on Francis Street in East Sydney. This formality was annoying; the two policemen already knew the answer. I wondered whether Benny was in some sort of trouble.

Early that morning a worker cutting the grass in the Botanical Gardens had found Benny's body near the Twin Ponds. The stab wound to his neck was most likely the cause of death, there was evidence of a struggle on the ground. The police found a bottle of brandy still half full under a tree near his body.

'Mr Anderson, do you have any information that can help with our investigation?'

I said that I was in my apartment the night before, unaware that Benny hadn't come home. No, I didn't know of anyone who could have got into a fight with Benny. The sergeant gave me a card with his name and phone number at the station.

After the police left, I stayed sitting. I recalled our conversation that day in Hyde Park when Benny warned me about being out there on my own. He was concerned about my safety and now this terrible news.

Nonna came over from behind the counter. When I told her that Benny had been murdered, she closed the front door and pulled up a chair next to me. She didn't ask for more information, and we cried in silence.

The next morning there was a firm, almost demanding knock on my door. It was Sergeant Carter, this time with a man in a grey suit with a yellow tie. Carter introduced the other man as a detective, but I cannot remember his name. 'Another homeless man' gave himself up at the Kings Cross police station early that morning. My first thought was how convenient a label 'homeless man' had become.

The man who'd handed himself over was Travis Dawson. The same character who I'd met a couple of years ago when he spoilt my privacy in Cooper Street Reserve. At the time I marked him down as a bullshitter but never a murderer.

The detective added that Dawson confessed he knew Benny had cash on him from the casual job and that's how the fight started. There was a knife involved, a fatal wound to Benny's neck meant he lost too much blood. Afterwards Dawson took three twenty-dollar notes and a few coins from Benny's trouser pocket.

Chloe's little car with dents on the bonnet veers left off the highway into Wentworth Avenue, glancing at her phone on the console between us, she says, 'We haven't got far to go now.'

I stare ahead until we see the tall white gable above the gates of the Memorial Park.

Outside a building with a sign on the lawn that says South

Chapel, a white minibus is parked next to three other cars. A group of people, most of them dressed in black, start moving through the heavy double doors, while Chloe pulls in on the other side of the bus.

The mourners take up chairs in the rows nearest to the coffin. Chloe sits close to me, her arm hooked into mine. I glance down at her knee-length black skirt and the matching Doc Martins boots. Nonna, her daughter Francesca and Mario are in the row behind us; I can hear the two women sniffing.

Silence creeps across the room; the pastor doesn't use the microphone. He coughs a couple of times before he glances at the coffin. On top of it there is a framed black-and-white photograph of Benny, taken outside the chapel in Kings Cross.

He starts by reassuring Benny he is not alone; that we are here today because we are proud to be his friends, always. 'Let us pray,' the pastor says as he clutches his hands together. He bows his head, and after the prayer, looks up with a smile.

'Our mate had a wonderful sense of humour. We all know about his habit of wearing odd pairs of socks. When I asked him about that at our Christmas lunch, he said the other pair was in the wash.'

With a more serious face the pastor recalls the first time he offered to pray for Benny. He had dismissed the offer, instead wondering where God was when he needed him most.

'Benny Mansfield, your childhood was bleak, beyond what any of us can imagine, but you were determined to find your path in life. We admire you, mate, there will always be a special place for you in our hearts.

'To conclude our service today, I invite Chloe Bradshaw to come forward.'

Chloe's voice quivers, she says she has chosen an old-time song, a song she hopes will connect with our friend Benny. When she reaches the final chorus of 'We'll meet again', behind her the curtain closes slowly on Benny's life.

On the drive back to the city we are quiet until Chloe asks, 'Are you okay, Dad?'

'I'm just thinking how Benny gave so much more than the scraps of life that came his way. Also, that you and I wouldn't be here together without him.' I lean forward, both hands covering my face.

My mother's recipe

I spend my days after Benny's funeral in dangerous territory, walking the streets alone, passing through neighbourhoods I don't recognise, lost and confused, wondering how I ended up there. I arrive at the soup kitchen late in the evening, searching for anyone I know. I leave without a meal.

On a weekday afternoon, I rest in a small park near a swing and seesaw for little ones. A girl with a blonde ponytail lifts her younger brother onto the seesaw. When she gets on the young fellow is too light and he is stuck in midair. It is only a few metres from where I am sitting on the bench, so I walk over and offer to help. While pushing down one end of the seesaw I notice the folds on the boy's chubby arms, for a moment I enjoy the fondest memory of Chloe as a toddler. My helping hand is interrupted when the mother shouts, 'Annabelle, Jamie, come back here, right now!' I'm shocked by the panic in her voice. She grabs the hands of her two children. I watch as they cross the road and then walk through the gate of a ground-floor townhouse. I remain standing at the seesaw; my embarrassment fades away to sadness.

One night the four walls of the apartment close in on me. After walking for hours, just meandering, I sit down in a bus shelter on Taylor Square. It is a part of the city that never goes quiet. Impatient drivers lean on their horns, shrill voices find their way home when others are already heading to work. I ignore the foul-mouthed tantrums, some possibly in my direction; ambulances race past with sirens and flashing lights.

I roll my brown woollen jumper into a tight bundle for a pillow. My last meal was a plate of oats for breakfast, but I am not thinking of food. With my back turned away from the busy intersection, I wrestle with Benny's warning, the first night I joined him in his shelter on Martin Place. 'Mate, isolation is the enemy of life,' he said.

I wake with a fright, there's a firm hand with strong fingers on my shoulder, I'm relieved to see a council worker in an orange vest. He says he just wanted to check whether I was still alive. I am cold and stiff, with that familiar foul taste in my mouth. At first light I start walking along Bourke Street in the opposite direction from my apartment. I should be at Nonna's for opening at seven o'clock, but I decide to keep walking, into an empty day.

Nonna must have let Chloe know that I didn't come to work. When I walk down Francis Street that afternoon, I see her sitting on the steps outside the front door. She doesn't say anything about me missing the shift, just that she had the afternoon free and decided to visit to say hello.

On the days when I don't help at Nonna's shop Chloe knocks on my door early. We go for long, lazy walks; she leads the way. There are reminders of Benny's absence everywhere; in the city parks, on empty benches, at street corners with the ticking sound of the pedestrian crossing, waiting our turn at drinking fountains. Some days Chloe just hangs around at my apartment. While I read a book from the community exchange on Riley Street, she sits on my bed with her legs drawn up and makes notes in pencil on her script. When my hair grows over my ears, she brings a pair of scissors in her canvas shoulder bag and cuts it for me. Every second week we take my sheets and towels to the laundry on Oxford Street. On my birthday she arrives with a framed photo of a sunrise at Bronte beach. From my bed, I can see the picture first thing in the morning.

My daughter's plan works; when Nonna asks about more shifts I think, Why not? I enjoy my time there, as long as there is no responsibility beyond selling and serving pies.

After the breakfast rush one morning I suggest my mother's favourite Shepherd's Pie as an addition to the menu. Nonna laughs at first but then she gives in. 'Okay, Davey boy, let's give it a try.'

The first small batch of the Shepherd's Pie is delicious, and I recommend it to every customer who comes into the shop.

Richo, the plumber from Burwood, is a three-pie regular and he gives it the thumbs up.

It's still fifteen minutes before opening time on the following Monday and already there is a line of customers waiting outside. I am busy sweeping under the communal table when Nonna calls me from the kitchen. The freshly baked pies in silver pans stretch the length of the bench, each pan with a yellow tag in her handwriting.

'David, today I needed to bake a second pan of your mother's recipe. I think they like it.'

Nonna wipes the perspiration from her eyes with her stained apron. I just smile and return to the front of the shop where the first customer in the queue, a bloke in a green Bunnings T-shirt, is knocking on the glass door.

Twin ponds

After a bowl of oats with berries I am waiting for Chloe outside the apartment block. I keep my eyes on a magpie above me on the powerline. My father believed if you showed magpies any aggression, they'd remember you and look for revenge. This may not be true and I've done this bird no harm, but I remain watchful.

I hear Chloe calling, 'Dad', and she waves from across the street. Always in the trademark boots, this morning she's wearing white shorts and an oversized cream-coloured jumper, her blonde hair just visible under a black peaked cap. I hesitate for a moment, to appreciate her from a distance.

Today is a year since Benny died. It was Chloe's idea to walk down to the Twin Ponds where they found his body. I am not sure what we'll do when we get there, but I agreed to come along. There are only a few cottonwool clouds in the sky and it feels like a good day to be alive as we walk along the road past the Art Gallery.

Once inside the Botanical Gardens, Chloe leads the way. I am wondering whether this was the route Benny chose on that day. He, and the man who killed him, must have been inside the gardens late afternoon because they lock the gates around sunset. Chloe stops on the footbridge where four white birds sit near the water's edge. When I catch up with her, she points to a tree to our right.

We walk closer and stand on the edge of the tall tree's circle of shade, with the sun on our backs, in silence. Chloe speaks first, and it is not what I expected.

'Dad, do you remember on the day of Benny's funeral, there was the program or run sheet or whatever they call it?'

'Yes, I have a copy in the apartment.' I am wondering whether she is trying to recall the verse from the bible chosen by the pastor.

'On the cover, below Benny's photograph, there was no date of birth. Just the day he died or was murdered.'

'Yes, now that you mention it.'

'Imagine coming to the end of your life and nobody knows when or where it started.'

I put my arm around Chloe, and she rests her head on my shoulder. Her body shakes as we stare at the spot where Benny spent his final night.

Suddenly I have a vivid image in my mind of Travis Dawson, the man who took Benny's life. In that first conversation in Cooper Street Reserve, he spoke without shame about his gambling addiction, driven by his desire to have more money. I am thinking how Travis Dawson allowed this ambition to become his whole life. He probably thought it was a good thing; that was all he could see. Out here such an addiction can flourish, and there was nobody to intervene, until he eventually killed a man for the handful of cash in his pocket. Dawson pleaded guilty, sentenced to fifteen years without parole. He will be an old man then. I wonder about his family; that is, if they still care. I don't say anything to Chloe about what I am thinking.

On the path leading to the Opera House, we stop to buy ice-creams from a young man with a cart under a blue-and-white striped umbrella. We find a bench facing the harbour, where we sit licking our vanilla ice-cream from cones.

'Is this the way it's going to be, Dad?'

Chloe's question is not in a demanding tone, I know exactly what she means.

'With your help, it feels that I'm putting my life together, slowly, one stitch at a time.'

She laughs and says, 'That's lovely, I mean the stitch part.'

We finish our ice-creams in silence, watching a ferry cross the expanse of calm water.

Chloe has an early afternoon rehearsal at the Sydney Theatre Company, I'd promised Nonna to be at the pie shop to help with the lunchtime rush. We decide on the shorter route back to my place along Macquarie Street. With her longer stride I am a step behind.

At the Bridge Street intersection, as we wait for the lights to change, Chloe points out the reflection of the morning sun from the glass and steel towers. She doesn't say anything. I wonder what's going through her mind right now; perhaps she's thinking how it is possible that a man can come down from those heights to a life on the street. I feel Chloe's closeness and the urge to take her hand.

Central Park West

My official address was West 73rd Street, one block from where John Lennon shared an apartment with the Japanese woman. When I first passed them on the reservoir wall, I thought, Here comes Jesus Christ and an angel in black. On that frosty night ahead of the early snow, the pay phone a few yards from my shelter rang for the first time since I'd moved to the city from Cooperstown in upstate New York. I turned over with my one good ear buried into the snot-stained pillow, but still I could hear the pleading call of the phone. Eventually I gave up. I hobbled across and picked up the black receiver.

'Hello, this is William A Wisniewski, my friends call me Billy.'

A male voice in an English accent, I would say a sophisticated English accent, asked whether I was on Central Park West. When I said, yes, this is where I live, the man asked whether it was true that John Lennon was dead.

'Yes, so sorry to bring you this news. Who am I speaking with?' I asked.

'My name is Ringo, a friend of John.' The English voice turned softer as if he were drifting away on a lazy river.

✦

I waited sixteen years for my next call. Once again it came after dark in winter. When I said, 'Hello, this is Billy Wisniewski speaking', a smoker's voice asked whether I was on Central Park West. 'I sure am, how can I help you?'

There was a brief pause and then the husky voice, now clearly tinged with emotion, asked, 'What are the celebrations like?'

I described how thousands of Yankees fans in navy and white bomber jackets, waving flags and blowing on plastic trumpets, had danced down the street on their way to Times Square. When my caller replied, 'Marvellous, our first world series in more than two decades' I knew it was him.

'Where have you been, Joe DiMaggio,' I asked.

Smoky hesitated, then the words I've been praying for. 'I'm right here, over on the East Side.'

'Thank the lord you haven't gone away,' I called out.

✦

It was a cloudless September morning. I had just fed the stale croissant crumbs from a Wendy's paper bag to a grey pigeon. Pedestrians took a wide berth with suspicious glances when they heard a payphone ring. A strange time of the day for somebody to call, it had to be urgent, so I picked up the black receiver.

'This is Billy Wisniewski on Central Park West. How can I help you?'

A high-pitched woman's voice screamed in my ear, 'Sweet Lord Jesus! Are you people safe up there?'

I said it was a pleasant day, everything was fine around here except for ambulances and fire trucks disturbing the peace, all of them heading south.

'That's where I am,' she shouted, so loud that I had to hold the receiver away from my good ear. 'The second tower is coming down, there are people flying like birds.'

Then the line went dead.

I stepped outside the phone booth; a dirty cloud rose above lower Manhattan.

✦

Without prior notice my payphone on West 73rd was removed while I was watching on from a bench on the sidewalk. A note from City Hall to explain why would have been nice, but then again, I should have known. The city was not the same anymore, the people around my place of residence had become richer and meaner. 'Sorry, I don't have any coins,' was the standard line as they took an odour-free detour around my 'A dime please' sign.

The man from AT&T had the decency to apologise when they loaded the booth onto the back of his truck. He said not many people used a landline these days.

I stood up, leaning on my crutch. I kept an eye on the blue-and-white logo until the truck disappeared around Columbus Circle. While I felt sad at that moment, even a little lonely, there would always be the memory of the last time my phone rang on West 73rd.

My final call was on an afternoon when a snowstorm turned daylight into sudden darkness. I was already inside the booth, my only chance for survival until the next morning. I struggled onto my knees before I could pick up the receiver, but the caller was patient.

'This is the Wisniewski residence on Central Park West,' I answered.

'Billy, is that you?'

The voice was soft and hesitant, almost as if the caller wanted to apologise before speaking. A shiver ran through my body like a full-on convulsion. The last time I'd heard that voice was the night the police came to our house.

I was at the table in the kitchen, just starting on my second pancake. Mama was at the stove, singing 'You are my sunshine' while she stirred corn soup in a black pot with her long wooden spoon. The front door slammed as if closed by a sudden wind gush. Daddy told me to get out, 'Get the fuck out of here.' When he turned around to face my mother, I saw he was holding a baseball bat behind his back. I was upstairs, under my bed, when the police came. The officer, with a thick black moustache and small ears tucked under his cap, had a gentle voice. 'Your mama is gone now. Come with us, you will be safe.'

In the Cooperstown orphanage they didn't really bother with birthdays, but my thick, swollen ankles and the craters in my back teeth reminded me that I was now on the wrong side of fifty. Here I was speaking to my mother's voice for the first time since that night in our kitchen, that would have been before Jack Kennedy died down in Texas.

'Yes, Mama, this is me, your Billy.'

'I've waited so long, Billy, praying, dreaming of the day when you will rest your head of curls on my chest again.'

'But, Mama, I thought, uh ... you know.'

'I understand, Billy, but that doesn't mean I have forgotten about you.'

'The policeman said my mama won't be coming back.'

'Billy, I have never been far away.'

Mama must have called from a landline because I didn't hear a beep for more coins. As the angry gale from the north blew drifts of snow under the glass door, my feet turned into numb blocks of ice. My conversation with Mama was interrupted when a slender woman in a full-length black coat with dark hair under a knitted black cap knocked on the door. I snarled at her like a wounded animal.

'Thank you, Mama,' I said. 'Thank you for finding me in this fucked-up maze infested with addicts and murderers and cat-size rats and maniacs driving on their horns.'

'I am so grateful, Billy boy, that I found you on your home number.'

'Mama, you called just when I was beginning to wonder.'

'What were you wondering, Billy boy?'

'Whether it would be easier for me to turn my back, Mama. I mean on this life.'

The line suddenly went quiet.

I asked, 'Mama, are you still there?'

She must have hung up. I left the receiver swinging on its twisted cord.

On Central Park West the city had turned off its lights early. I blinked but everything was black.

✦

A woman with intense brown eyes below her green surgical cap held my hand. The only sound in the room was the beeping of the machine on the other side of the bed.

She asked whether I could tell her my name. I spoke with a hoarse voice and said yes, she can call me Billy. I felt a bitter slime pushing up in my throat, and when I raised my head to cough, I saw a white bandage around my right foot, but my left foot was gone.

'Billy, I am Doctor Adler, you are in the Columbia Presbyterian Hospital.'

After the coughing fit, I felt desperately tired and closed my eyes.

I heard the doctor say that a woman had brought me to the hospital in the back of a taxi, two days ago; the woman left without leaving her name. Was there a home number or perhaps a family member she should phone? I pretended to be asleep.

A Stolen Moment

The kiss is long and soft. Not urgent, certainly not a farewell. Enough time for a single shutter release of my camera. I imagine I can still taste the sweetness of their kiss as the train reaches the end of the platform, before we disappear into a black tunnel. The yellow light in our compartment shines on young faces without expression. Ahead of us an uncertain journey to a land where we don't belong.

✦

The helicopter flies low over the trees. Suddenly there is a clearing and we swoop down on a village of bamboo huts. People run in all directions before bullets from our machine guns propel them face down into the mud. An old woman stumbles with a child in her arms. She turns to look up at the helicopter; they don't make it to the edge of the forest. By the time our chopper turns back towards base camp, flamethrowers light up the huts.

They are burning like candles on a birthday cake.

Inside my canvas purse the stolen moment is creased like an old newspaper clipping. A photograph with the promise that we'll go home when this is over, to people who care about us, to those who write letters about everyday privileges, like family gatherings, a homerun at the bottom of the ninth, a favourite recipe for Thanksgiving dinner, the first words of a sister's toddler; always the reassurance that you are loved and that they miss you.

In the jungle days feel like months, the birds don't sing. So quiet I only hear my own breathing and the squelch of rubber boots in the mud. The enemy's invisible but I know they are there. They wait patiently, defending their home. I am fighting, killing men who have done me no harm; then there are those too young or too old to fight, but they die anyway. I am here because my number came up in a lottery, so far from home I forget whether it lies to the east or the west.

We crouch while waiting for the signal, ahead lies no-man's land the length of a football field. A wave of the arm our silent command; keep your head down and sprint to the tree line. A firm grip of the automatic rifle, my index finger on the trigger. Running on the right-hand side of the V formation, I am flying through the air, the ringing in my ears.

'Down, stay down.' The voice echoes as if I'm inside an empty chamber.

Behind me a weak, 'Please help me.'

My legs are not hurting, then black as night.

The helicopter lands on the roof of a building, two men

with a red cross on their khaki uniforms carry me on a stretcher. Inside the swing door they lower me onto a bed with wheels, down the wide corridor people make way without taking notice. A young woman with brown eyes runs next to my bed with a bag of clear fluid. I see scorched chest hair where my undershirt has been cut open, a grey blanket with dark blood patches is wrapped around my legs. I can hear voices.

'We cannot waste any time,' one of them shouts.

I feel the needle in my arm, then there is a creeping darkness, just like the start of a feature film.

✦

War is over, both sides claim victory, we are going home, our commander promises a hero's welcome. Coffins draped in flags, others are left behind in unmarked graves. Generations scarred for life, refugees with nothing but the clothes they wear, fields and rivers stained with blood. Some preach the war was necessary, others pray this should never happen again.

'Give peace a chance,' they sing.

In the quiet of the night the tears of a widow, the anguish of a mother, and some too young to understand, only that Daddy isn't coming home.

It is spring back home, the sun shines with renewed optimism. The flags are at full stretch in a stiff breeze. Along the perimeter of the warship our heroes stand at attention. On the quay the temporary grandstand is packed with people shading their eyes against the morning glare, searching for a familiar face on deck.

The military band plays a battle hymn, the cue for those on board to salute. Before we reach the chorus I notice a crowd of thousands more outside the steel fence of the naval base. These people aren't singing, they are carrying banners and placards, no words of welcome. The largest banner is raised by a line of young women. 'KILLERS' it says in red letters on a white background, the ink running like blood.

Our ship gives the quay a gentle nudge, the instruction is for able men to disembark first, we need to show strength. Let's not forget this is a victorious homecoming. Eventually it is my turn. A nurse who introduces himself as Garcia pushes my wheelchair down the gangplank. Dockside, family members and soldiers embrace, a boy with a head of blond curls hangs on to his father's dark green military tunic.

At the bottom of the gangplank Garcia swings my wheelchair to where a row of ambulances wait, out of sight from the Welcome Home crowd.

Then I see them, her cheeks wet with tears as she bends down. He holds her face with both hands. The couple whose kiss I stole at the railway station, now almost three years ago, the promise of a safe return I hung onto as if it were my own, a photograph now lying in a field with fragments of my flesh and bone.

The History Lesson

The sun has just peeped over North Head, and the water shines like a giant mirror. From where we sit on a flat rock we watch as two yachts with white sails crawl towards Watsons Bay, the air is cool but there is the promise of summer heat. In the red gum behind us two kookaburras engage in lively conversation.

We left home early, allowing Catherine to sleep in on her day off from the hospital. I can't help but smile at the way my son closes his eyes when biting on his bacon and egg roll. I love this boy; it's hard to believe that in a couple of months we'll celebrate his thirteenth birthday. His uncombed brown curls fall over the collar of his navy jumper. I move closer and put my arm around his shoulder.

With our breakfast treat finished Damien and I climb down to the water's edge. He points to a rock. 'Dad, what's that?'

I shade my eyes with one hand against the rising sun and see an anchor attached to a chain. When I bend forward I realise the rusted anchor is secured against the rock with a steel bracket. Damien is right next to me. Carrying a puzzled frown, he bends down to have a closer look.

'Hey, do you think it's been here for a very long time?'

'It's hard to tell, son. It is old and rusty. But look at the steel bracket fixed to the rock; looks like someone did that not so long ago.'

'But, Dad, why would anyone want to keep it here?'

I feel under pressure to come up with a feasible story to explain why a rusted ship's anchor would be secured to a rock on the shore of Sydney Harbour. The look on Damien's face suggests that his brain is racing through numerous possibilities. It is when in this dreaming, wondering mood that he has a habit of rubbing the tip of his nose with the palm of his hand.

'Okay, mate, I think this is what could have happened here.' I sit down on the nearest rock, facing my son.

'Like our family, there are thousands of Australians who are directly related to people who arrived on those first ships that sailed into the harbour, more than 200 years ago.'

'Was that what they call the First Fleet, Dad, in 1788?'

'Exactly, you are pretty good with your history. And it was on this day, 26th of January.'

I pause to appreciate this moment with my clever son, our only child.

'But, Dad, that's so long ago. It couldn't have lasted all that time.'

'You're right, but perhaps a person related to one of those First Fleet families came back here, just recently, to attach this anchor to the rock. Like us, so many people are proud of their First Fleet connection.'

Damien looks at me with a faraway expression and there it is again, rubbing his noise vigorously with the palm of his left hand.

'So, it's like a symbol? Like, this is where our family first landed on this new land.'

'That's right, son. This is where it all started.'

Damien has turned and is looking back up the leafy embankment where we ate our bacon and egg rolls.

'Dad, when our family arrived here on those ships, what about the people who already lived here? On this land, I mean.' He waves his arm across the bush behind us.

'I think there was a bit of trouble in the beginning, but the captain of the fleet sorted it out. Remember they came from England; they were the only ones here with guns.'

'Okay, so those people who lived here forever weren't too happy but our families were more powerful.' His frown remains as if it is painted on.

'And that, my boy, is the whole story. Today we celebrate the beginning of Australia, the country we are so proud of.'

My story must have lost its appeal because Damien stands up and starts walking towards the carpark.

'Mum's probably waiting for us,' he says over his shoulder.

✦

Catherine stacks Damien's plate with lamb chops and thick farmer's sausage from the barbeque, leaving little room for the oven baked chips or beetroot salad. Following the grace, we touch our glasses filled with a deep red McLaren Vale shiraz. Across the table Damien is already chewing on his first bite of the sausage.

'Dad says you guys had a good time down at Middle Harbour this morning.'

With his mouth full we have to wait for an answer.

'It was fun, Dad and I were the only people down there. We had bacon and egg rolls, with sauce. Then Dad gave me a bit of a history lesson.'

'You mean about the public holiday, about Australia Day?'

'Yeah, about the First Fleet when our family, or Dad's family, arrived in Australia.'

'Oh, that would have been interesting. What did Dad tell you?'

I take a long sip of the shiraz, listening to our son as he talks about the anchor we found near the water.

'Dad thinks it could have been left there by someone whose family came with the First Fleet.'

'Well, that's a possibility.' Catherine leans forward to show she is really interested in his story.

'Yeah, then Dad told me about that day when the First Fleet arrived in the harbour. The local people waited for them on the shore and there was a bit of an argument.'

'You mean between the people who arrived on the first ships and the people who already lived here?'

'Yeah, Mum, the people weren't happy about these invaders but the men on the ships had guns they brought from England.'

Catherine looks at me with a questioning expression, while Damien continues with his story.

'But that was only the beginning. After that day the Australians, you know the Aboriginal people, wanted to protect their land, the land they lived on all their lives. Lots of them were murdered by our people, with guns.'

'And Dad told you all of this today, when you went down to the harbour for breakfast?'

Catherine's question is meant for me, but I remain silent and refill my glass of wine.

'Yeah, Mum, and he told me about the children too.'

My right leg jumps under the chequered tablecloth.

'What about the children, Damien?' Catherine turns towards him; this is now a conversation that leaves me as the spectator.

'Our people, like the ones who came on those ships into Sydney Harbour, they took Aboriginal children away from their families.'

I feel helpless as our son continues with his version of my story.

'They took the children away to schools, to schools like mine where we have uniforms and morning prayer.'

With that Damien pushes his chair back and says, 'Excuse me from the table.'

✦

When I walk into his bedroom Damien is at the trestle table, his left elbow resting on a sketch pad with a pencil in his right hand. Over his shoulder I see a drawing of what looks like a eucalyptus tree, almost bare.

'Can I talk to you for a moment?' I put my hand on his shoulder.

'Sure, Dad,' he says as his pencil hovers above the drawing.

'The story you told Mum, that's not really what I told you this morning.'

'I know.'

He can be a little rascal, I think.

'So, who told you about the Aboriginal people being murdered? And the children?'

Damien puts the pencil down and turns around to look me in the eye.

'Grandma Russo told me.'

'But your grandma –'

Damien interrupts me.

'She told me that last afternoon in the hospital. Remember the day I went to say goodbye, when you and Mum were talking to the doctor outside her room.'

'Why do you think she did that?'

'Grandma said she wanted me to know the true history of Australia. She spoke so softly that I had to lean in, close to her face.'

'Was that all? Did Grandma Russo say anything else that day in the hospital?'

Damien's dark eyes seem hesitant, avoiding my gaze.

'She said you might be upset when you find out, Dad.'

'Upset about what she told you?' I concentrate on keeping

my response soft, not demanding an answer.

'Not just about the murders and the children, Dad.'

'Mate, I won't get upset, please tell me what else Grandma told you.'

'Grandma took both my hands and then she said her grandmother, something about her mother's side, was taken away from her family. By the police.'

My son turns around and picks up the coloured pencil. I watch as he starts drawing the outline of another brown leaf falling to the red earth below the eucalyptus tree.

✦

Catherine has cleared our plates by the time I walk outside again. Sitting down opposite her, I can hear the nightlife stirring in the trees. My glass is empty, but I don't feel like more wine. In the discomfort of my own silence, I think about how my version of the Australian story has been rewritten on this night.

Catherine uses a paper napkin to dab her eyes. I remember when, as a young mother, she sat in the lounge room with soaked tissues in her fist. Heartbroken by images on television of Aboriginal girls being dragged away from their families. For me it was a slice of history, dramatically reimagined by a Hollywood director.

When I reach across the table for her hand she stands up and takes the empty chair next to me, where our son left his glass, still half full with apple juice.

I break the suffocating silence, my voice is croaky. I share word for word the conversation I just had with Damien. When

I mention his drawing of the bare eucalyptus tree with its leaves on the red soil, Catherine says he has spoken recently, on several occasions, about what he has learned at school, about Aboriginal people's relationship with their land, with this land.

'Did you know, before today, that your mother told Damien?'

Catherine nods and leans her head against my shoulder. 'I'm not surprised. She believed in him.'

Tale of the Goatherd

In the El-Bariyah I am on my own, but I don't feel alone. There is always the presence of a desert mirage, an image of wonder that moves when it stands still. I sharpen my eyes into narrow slits and the mirage takes shape, as if it is being drawn by a lazy painter. I see the outline of an ancient rock, part of this Judean Desert since the day Abraham walked down to the Dead Sea. Beyond the rock stands a wise old tree, not ashamed by its nakedness, roots thirsty since it rained for forty days and forty nights, a time before my first breath.

My eyes wander across this landscape of nothing. A puff of yellow grass peeps through the crust of dry soil, spread thin like the growth on my chin. You won't hear me complaining, not from a herdsman blessed with two desert-dwelling goats, both brown as the earth with one white leg, not the same leg, they look the perfect companions. When the sun sits on the edge of the earth there will be a tin of milk in one of those udders, as long as I remain patient. A slow and gentle squeeze, one udder at a time, enough milk to help me swallow the chunk of barley bread. I am partial to sundried locusts, deliciously crispy with the heads and tails removed. Then a fistful of juicy olives to finish off my daily feast.

The sun is dipping towards the sandstone mountain in the west. I let the goats wander a while longer. I think I see two smaller trees. No, the mirages are moving towards me, with a steady stride, there is purpose in the way they move. The goats turn around before cantering in my direction, ever alert to warn me against potential danger. The mirages are now sharper. I can see arms moving, thick, dark hair swaying in the desert breeze. Close enough now for my old watery eyes to see two women. They walk with the sameness of sisters. Suddenly they stop, as if on command, and the one on the left waves with her right hand. I raise my herder stick cut from a fallen tobacco tree. The woman on the right waves with her left hand.

I use the stick to struggle into a standing position. The two women are walking again, in a straight line to where I stand with my hunched back. I shuffle towards them, followed by my two loyal goats. The women hold their chins in the pride position, we are now close enough for me to throw a stone. Behind me I hear the '*Blehhhh*' of the older goat, always the cautious one. The women stop, I can see the lashes of their identical dark eyes.

'My name is Dawud, are you looking for someone out here?'

The women shake their heads, slowly as if to say, 'We are not in a hurry.'

'Halima,' says the one on the left.

'Ayelet,' says the one on the right.

I thought they were sisters, but now I know my first impression was one of a fool. Why would a Palestinian woman walk in the El-Bariyah with a Hebrew woman? I wonder, loud enough for them to hear. This is something rarer than water mixing with dust out in this desert.

'We share pain from wounds you cannot see, old herder,' says the Hebrew woman, Ayelet. 'My friend Halima and I come out here to mourn our two younger brothers.'

'If they are younger, why should they be mourned,' I said.

Ayelet looks at Halima before Halima looks at Ayelet.

'Our brothers died on the same hour at the same place.' Halima answers in a whisper that screams in the desert silence. 'I met Ayelet the day after, together on hands and knees, searching through the rubble that once was the school, digging with our bare hands, for something, anything, to remember our brothers, a book with his name, a shoe, the ring on a finger, a piece of clothing we may recognise. We cried. I said a prayer in her language.' Halima swallows and looks at her Hebrew companion.

'Ayelet held my hands, people turned away, others spat on us. In that moment of hopelessness, the wailing of mothers almost unbearable, we made a promise, that we will walk into this desert, walk side by side, to pray together, pray for our children, for our fathers who seek revenge, pray for the soil we share, to be peaceful like this life in the El-Bariyah.'

The Hebrew woman moves closer, and Halima takes her hand.

'Out here, away from the smell of death, in a place where the odour of dry blood doesn't fill our nostrils, we see one another. We understand even when we speak with different tongues. With you, old soul, and your two goats, as our guardians, to keep us safe with your watchful eye.'

I stare at the women with silent gratitude that I am blessed with this ordinary life. A life I chose when I was no more than a boy, away from home, as far as these knees could carry my thin body, to this empty spread of earth's surface. The desert sand, swept by a howling wind from the west, would have covered my footsteps. The goats don't care where I came from, what brought me here, to this existence, of so little but not lacking in anything.

Ayelet the Jew and Halima from Palestine, two sisters from two mothers, turn to face one another with open palms, their foreheads touch as they look down at their feet, in the desert soil. The two women embrace, whispering prayers, then silence. They turn away, slowly, as if they are clinging to this moment. They start walking, towards Jerusalem. The sun is lower now, almost ready to say goodbye, the goats have gone ahead. I follow, leaning on my herder's stick, over my shoulder the two fading mirages move with the same rhythm. I hope for Ayelet and Halima there will be a tomorrow, together under this one sky.

Sitting in the mouth of my cave, I rest my back against the warm, rough face of the rock, the moon is somewhere else tonight. In the blackness the goats stir, my sleepy thoughts drift to the two women, who walked into my desert life this afternoon. Halima and Ayelet. I cannot know their pain, like the point of a white-hot sword, driven into their hearts. Two brothers, only boys, both gone. I now hear their voices, Halima's courage. 'It was my brother, who carried the bomb.'

Ayelet refusing to give in to hatred. Somewhere, deep inside, she found a little light, of forgiveness.

Cape of Good Hope

Sorcha Mannion

I grew up on the Connemara when there were more gravestones than people in our village. My father was the gravedigger; everyone trusted him to dig a final resting place deep enough for the soul of a loved one. For miles under the ever-present blanket of fog we knew everyone; perhaps more than that, we were probably all related.

'I go to more funerals than weddings on this peninsula,' my mother used to complain when ironing her black dress.

Beyond the bogs, the heathland and funerals, my most vivid recollection of my early life on the Connemara was the hunger. I became aware of the dull, ever-present grip around my stomach before I started school, and it stayed with me until the damp spring morning when I hugged my mother outside the heavy door of the convent in Galway.

My decision to become a nun didn't feel selfish, although

the promise of a regular meal was persuasive. In truth, it wasn't my decision at all. Father and Mother spoke to me kindly, they waited until my sisters and brothers were asleep while we remained at the kitchen table. Mother held my hand; Father rested his palms on the bible.

'Our family needs the bed with the arrival of your sibling, now there will be eight of you. And, Sorcha, the money from digging graves isn't enough to feed all the mouths under our roof,' Father said in a whisper.

I waved farewell to Galway Bay on a morning with a pale autumn sky. By then my nun's habit disguised a body where you could no longer count the ribs below my ample bosom.

'God be with you,' my mother said, as she clutched a handkerchief in her small fist.

I stood near the stern of the freight ship. With dry cheeks I watched as rain and heavy clouds closed across the Connemara coastline.

It was dockside in Southampton, holding on to my small brown suitcase, where I met Sister Brigid. She was taller than me, by at least a loaf of bread, with a perfect set of front teeth, the strong hands of a man and her breath smelled of whisky.

The sailor in black uniform at the top of the gangway raised a loud hailer and called, 'All aboard.'

Sister Brigid and I, my name had now changed to Sister Frances, shared a cabin with two bunks and a small window just above the water line on the fifteen-day passage to Cape Town.

Patricia Byrne

My father taught me to play the fiddle; that was before I discovered the Irish bouzouki. Unlike my father, I had a terrible singing voice. He often joked that I sounded like a donkey being strangled. This didn't stop us performing in bars across the north side of old Dublin town. He was proud to be joined by his oldest girl on the bouzouki.

'Folks, introducing Liam and Patricia Byrne!'

By the time we played 'The Fields of Athenry' there were enough coins in Father's grey hat for another pint. This meant he was happy, and he sang another few tunes as we walked home.

Daddy went without saying goodbye; the postman found his body on a bench near the factory gate, clutching his lunch box and coffee flask. Doctor Doyle said Daddy wouldn't have suffered, it was instant. The suffering was left to his wife and six children in our terrace house without heating and brown water stains on the ceiling. The dinner stew was never enough to go around the table, with just gravy left in the pan for me to mop up with a slice of brown bread.

Father O'Neill came to the house when my mother was still dressed in black, offering the comfort of a prayer. He made the most of the void Daddy left. In the stillness of the night I could hear the rhythmic creaking of my mother's bed and then her, 'Yes, Father, yes, Father.'

When the priest invited me to become a nun, I didn't hesitate. I so longed for a decent night's sleep without the farting of my two younger brothers and a plate of porridge in the morning, perhaps even a slice of bread with butter and

Chivers strawberry jam.

My family stood in a line on the sidewalk for a final wave before Father O'Neill drove me to the port of Dublin in his two-door Hillman. It was a week after my nineteenth birthday, I was now Sister Brigid.

When he whispered, 'Go well, my child' with a brush of his lips on my cheek, I remained calm and said, 'Farewell, you dirty old bastard.'

On the dock in Southampton our nuns gathered away from the other passengers waiting for the call to board. I noticed a face with sad blue eyes and blonde strands showing from under the wimple. With a small suitcase in hand, she stood a few steps away from the other nuns who were in hushed conversation. This girl must have noticed me staring and smiled before coming across with an outstretched hand.

'Sister Frances, from Connemara,' she introduced herself. I figured she was a few years older than me.

Sister Frances

We sailed into Table Bay on a cloudless day except for a little white puff falling down the granite face of the mountain. This view of Table Mountain was more beautiful than the picture hanging on the wall of the ship's dining room. The bay was calm, a school of dolphins swam in the wake of the *Pendennis Castle*, like a welcoming party.

From our new home in the suburb of Philippi we could no longer see the ocean, but the mountain stood like a watchful parent over its flock. The convent, with its small, stone-walled chapel, was attached to a girls' high school where Sister Brigid and I were the only nuns among the teaching staff. I was assigned English and geography as my subjects, while Sister Brigid taught music and conducted the choir; on Wednesday afternoons, she took charge of the tennis lessons. Through the window of my classroom, I watched Sister Brigid chasing after the ball in her knee-length black habit and white tennis shoes.

Saturdays the school ground was deserted and we spent the afternoon in the convent garden with its old vine-covered pergola. Sister Brigid played the guitar from the school's music room and I sang along, first on my own and then towards the bottom of the whisky flask she would join me for our favourite, 'The Rising of the Moon'.

The shade of the wild fig tree was a perfect spot for an afternoon nap. I loved her in a way the Lord didn't prepare me for, perhaps more so after they came for us in the blackness of midnight.

Sister Brigid

Our ship docked at the Cape of Good Hope when the apartheid law was still a work in progress. Our mission was to save souls among those disadvantaged by a sheet of paper that made whites the superior race. The girls in our school had smooth, dark olive skin. They didn't seem to care about our snow-white complexions above the round collars of the habits, the only pale faces among their teachers.

Sister Frances and I didn't talk much about life on the shores of Ireland. From that first morning, dockside in Southampton, the Lord walked ahead of us on this journey, towards a new horizon. At school we watched our girls grow into confident young women with hope in their eyes.

When I went down on my knees next to the bed, I said thank you for this life, a life that as a child I didn't know was possible. Certainly not the closeness and gentle touch of Sister Frances, or Sorcha from Connemara, the name I prefer.

It started on the inside pages of the newspapers, only single column reports, then came photographs of buildings going up in flames, breaking news of police shooting at children, the prime minister warns with an angry snarl, military vehicles with armed soldiers join the morning traffic, elders call for calm. The young are prepared to pay the ultimate price, traitors get punished with burning tyres around their necks. Schools are not spared, the headmistress says please be careful, make sure your door is locked at night.

Sorcha and I pray for those seeking retribution, fuelled by their dignity denied. We also remember the minority, who are fearful. On this night, together, with the quilted bed cover pulled over our heads, we hear chanting, angry voices, banging on the front door of the convent, windows being smashed. We hold on to one another, clinging to our final breath, as the fire sucks the air through the door of our bedroom.

✦

Father Matheson remains silent as his gaze sweeps across the assembly hall. Every seat is taken, the younger girls stand along the back wall on either side of the double doors.

'On Wednesday night our community was the target of a violent demonstration, sadly by young men whose anger should have been directed elsewhere. The heroic effort of a parent, on his way home from working a night shift, saved the lives of two teachers at our school. For this selfless deed William Jansen was prepared to risk his own life.' There is a quiver in the priest's booming voice.

'He ran into the burning convent twice, first for Sister Frances, then he managed to drag Sister Brigid to safety before the roof collapsed. During my visit to the hospital yesterday, I mentioned to the two teachers that we plan to gather for a special assembly. Their wish was for us to pray for William Jansen and his family, but not to forget the demonstrators in our prayers. This consideration, from two people with horrific injuries, facing a slow, painful recovery, made me feel small.'

He raises his arms and asks the assembly to join him in prayer.

Following his 'Amen', Father Matheson's sombre face relaxes into a smile.

'There was a further request for today's assembly, this was from Sister Brigid, still with her mischievous streak. She asked for the school choir to please sing "Red is the Rose", a song they have rehearsed on several occasions in class. My homework suggests this is an Irish folk song that tells the tale of a love that's fairer than any.'

He turns towards the girl at the piano, who plays a few bars before she nods at the school choir gathered to her left on the stage.

The choir girls hold hands as they start to sing, some with their eyes closed, and sway gently to the high-pitched melody of Sister Brigid's request.

Shadow of the Flat Top Mountain

Faith in our leader, June 1977

It was the week leading up to the annual intervarsity rugby match. Claire Rosen, who had been a year ahead of me at the same girls' high school in Johannesburg, had the directions to a student share house away from the university campus. She asked me not to mention this to anyone else in my residence.

The intervarsity was a rivalry against an Afrikaans-speaking university that went back almost a hundred years. On that day students in their team colours gathered in the stands to sing and chant until they were hoarse. Leading the supporter groups on opposite sides of the stadium were cheerleaders in colourful cloaks with matching top hats.

I decided not to attend the supporters 'sing-song' practice on campus this evening. Instead, following Claire's instructions, I made my way to the sports fields, a five-minute walk from the women's residence. The night was black, a strong north westerly wind pushed heavy clouds down the slopes of Table Mountain.

Our group of six girls huddled on the concrete steps of the open grandstand. The first big drops started falling on our plastic raincoats while Claire, keeping her voice low, explained the plan for the evening.

She led the way down the hill in driving rain to a bus stop on Main Road, the major thoroughfare through the southern suburbs of Cape Town. From there we took a city bound bus to Rosebank, where Claire asked the driver to stop at the post office.

Two guys, student friends of Claire's, were waiting for us. In the deluge we didn't bother with introductions, but I heard Claire calling the shorter guy in a hooded rain jacket 'Andy'. The wind blew our umbrellas to ruin as we followed her along a narrow street, till she stopped at the first cross street.

'Why are we waiting here?' I asked her, in a whisper.

'We need to make sure nobody is following us.'

Outside a white-washed cottage with an overgrown front garden Claire raised her hand. She opened the gate, which was hanging skew on its hinges. Our group stood closely together under a canvas canopy as she knocked twice on the front door, waited a few seconds, and knocked four times. There were footsteps inside on a wooden floor, a male voice asked, 'Claire?'

The man who opened the door wasn't someone I recognised

from campus. He wore a brown knee-length woollen coat over a matching rollneck jersey, a black beret rested slightly skew on his dark curls. Inside, we left puddles of water on the floor when we took off our raincoats. Behind me I heard the key in the lock and then a chain being hooked into position.

We followed the man with the beret down the passage to what looked like a lounge room without furniture and a counter to an open-plan kitchen. Eight other people were already in the room, I assumed all students. Bean bags were spread around on the floor in a half-moon, and closer to the kitchen counter was a small round table with two white plastic chairs. I felt a little apprehensive as we stood around, waiting to help ourselves to mugs of instant coffee with condensed milk out of a can.

Some of us shared bean bags while the guy who opened the door remained standing at the kitchen counter. He had removed his coat and placed the beret next to him on the small table.

With a mug of coffee in his left fist our host said, 'Okay, let's get started. For those of you I haven't met before, my name is Steven Mbeki. I am a law student in my fourth year, in the same class as Andy Gibson.'

Without the woollen coat this man had a lean and athletic body; his closely cropped black beard showed off the whiteness of his perfect teeth. His accent was English second language, like the other Black students I have met on campus.

'It would be nice if we can go around the room and introduce ourselves. Please don't be shy, let's get to know one another, we are in this together. Why don't we start with my friend serving the coffee tonight?'

The guy behind the kitchen counter in a grey track suit and uncombed light brown hair introduced himself as Ryan Plimsoll, the son of an apple farmer. He was studying engineering and shared the house with Steven Mbeki. We all laughed when he said that he didn't have much luck with girls.

In her introduction Claire thanked everyone from the residence who came out on a night with such lousy weather. She referred to Steven Mbeki and Andy Gibson as 'my comrades in the fight against discrimination'.

Claire Rosen had wild, shoulder-length brown curls. Her dark blue eyes demanded that you didn't look away. At school she was the head girl and leader of our team in the debating contest. As a student in political studies, she contributed regularly to the student newspaper, never shying away from controversial opinion. Our families knew one another in the Jewish community but we weren't close friends. Claire and I met up again in the university residence.

We learned that Andy first studied at the University of Natal in Durban before he transferred to Cape Town in his second year. He lived on campus, a short walk away from Claire and my residence. His honey blond hair curled over his ears, he wore round silver-framed glasses and a khaki shirt buttoned to the top.

As the introductions continued, I figured out I was probably the youngest in the group. My turn came last, this gave me a little more time to decide how best to introduce myself.

'Hi, everyone, I am Rebecca Kaplan, I study architecture and I'm in my second year. Claire invited me along this evening.

I was a bit nervous when we made our way here, but now I look forward to getting to know you better. Thank you for including me.'

'That's nice, Rebecca.' Steven was leaning against the kitchen counter.

✦

It was after midnight when our group left the house, the rain had stopped, the streetlights were brighter, stormwater still thundered down the gutters. Claire reminded us to be quiet as we walked to the bus stop, along a different route this time. My head was spinning with Steven's plan for the next day, his casual but confident demeanour and his hand on my forearm as we said goodnight at the front door.

Back at the residence I first went to Claire's room. We left our raincoats dripping in the shower. Claire stood puffing on a rolled cigarette at the window only slightly opened. Outside it was raining again heavily.

She went over our plan to interrupt lectures immediately after the lunch break. We had Steven's reassurance that our group, who'd met at the house in Rosebank, would be joined by other protesters. We would take the authorities by surprise, not giving campus security time to intervene.

I struggled to fall asleep as I contemplated protesting against the killing of those defenceless children. It has been a year since the uprising in Soweto, a black township south of Johannesburg. The schoolkids protested about Afrikaans as a compulsory language, the police response was brutal. They fired live rounds, there were reports of kids shot in the back; the youngest was a twelve-year-old boy. There has never been retribution.

From tomorrow that would change and I would be part of it. I had faith in our leader Steven Mbeki; he gave the impression that he would lead by example.

✦

By Tuesday morning the storm off the Atlantic Ocean had subsided, there was a glimpse of blue sky. I made my way to the first lecture, walking with students from the university residences, others were disembarking from a line of buses. The friendly chatter and students scurrying around like ants appealed to me, I loved this life on campus.

The night before Claire had suggested that we should meet after the second lecture at the student canteen. We sat in a sunny spot on the stairs outside, sipping from mugs of tea, when Steven Mbeki approached us from across the courtyard, again wearing the brown coat and black beret.

'Hey, Claire, morning, Rebecca, how are you today?'

I was pleased that he remembered my name. Steven sat down on the stairs close enough for me to feel his physical presence. It seemed a habit for him to place a hand on your shoulder or touch your elbow when he spoke to you.

'So, our day has come.' He clapped his hands together. 'I am catching up with Andy during the lunch break; the two of us will be together in the first lecture this afternoon.'

I looked at Claire and she must have noticed my frown.

'Rebecca, you won't be on your own. We have commitments

from other students in your class.'

Steven left Claire and me on the steps with a 'Let's do it' before he walked away in the direction of the law faculty.

As per his plan, at exactly 2.15 that afternoon groups of students, each about twenty strong, stood up in eight classrooms spread across campus and started chanting, 'Justice for the children.' Some lecturers simply sat down to allow the students to continue with the protest, while Dr Bradbury in my class collected his notes and left in a hurry, almost as if he was concerned for his safety.

The university authorities were clearly taken by surprise. By mid-afternoon a crowd of students, I thought five hundred, maybe more, had left their lectures and gathered on the steps leading up to the tall pillars of the administration building. Steven stood on the top step and used a hand-held loud haler to address the crowd. I took a position against the pillar to his left.

Our leader first asked for a minute's silence as a show of respect for the young people who were gunned down by police in Soweto on this day a year ago. I stood with my eyes closed as the buzz of the crowd faded into absolute silence; I could hear the traffic on the freeway below the campus. Then Steven thanked us all.

'What started as a peaceful protest by school children turned into a bloodbath. It's been a year in which we've had promises and more promises for a thorough inquest, but clearly that was just to pacify the international community. Enough of that, my friends, let us stand up and be heard, across this land.'

Steven raised his fist and the crowd repeated after him the

chant, '*Amandla*' and again '*Amandla*.' The chilling cry for 'power' in the Xhosa language echoed from the stone walls of the campus buildings.

A tall blond man in a grey suit with dark-framed glasses resting on a hooked nose suddenly appeared next to Steven. I wasn't close enough to hear their conversation, but the man seemed agitated and pointed his finger at Steven as he spoke.

The crowd became restless; some chanted 'Justice for the children', while others towards the back started whistling and booing. A girl behind me said the man was the vice-chancellor. I saw Steven hand over the loud haler to the university official.

'I appeal to all of you here this afternoon to please disperse peacefully. We respect your right to protest, but disruption of lectures like what happened across the campus today cannot be tolerated.' He paused when the crowd started booing again.

'As discussed with this gentleman here, there are other avenues to demonstrate your sympathy for those who lost their lives a year ago. This should not be received as a threat, but the university authorities must act in the best interests of all students on campus.'

With that the vice-chancellor handed the loud haler back to Steven and disappeared through the double doors of the administration building. Some students started moving away towards the classrooms, but most of the crowd remained as Steven called for attention.

'Before we leave campus this afternoon, I hope we never forget those who paid the ultimate price by standing up for a basic right. The right to be educated in their mother tongue rather than the language of their oppressors.'

I was taken by surprise when Claire stepped forward to take the loud haler.

'This is bullshit. We can't have education as usual in an abnormal society.' The crowd cheered and when Claire raised her fist, we repeated her call of, '*Amandla, Amandla.*'

A student with black hair long enough to cover the collar of his denim jacket pointed at the highway below the campus. I could see the blue flashing lights of a police convoy taking the exit to the university.

Steven grabbed the loud haler from Claire and shouted, 'Don't move, don't move.'

✦

The light was fading on the university side of the mountain; I could feel the early warning of a cold night creeping through my windbreaker. The crowd of students had dispersed. I sat on the steps of the administration building with Claire and Andy Gibson.

'Do you realise the police arrived just minutes after the vice-chancellor addressed the crowd?' It was Andy who broke the silence.

'You're right, that does seem suspicious.' Claire couldn't hold back her frustration. 'I can't believe that most of the students just ran away when the police jumped out of their vans; after all the brave chanting beforehand.'

I wanted to confess that I was terrified when I saw the police with those vicious German shepherd dogs, but I didn't say anything. I felt weak, like an imposter. Claire and Andy with two other students who confronted the police had their names and addresses taken.

'This doesn't feel like a time for celebration, but I could do with a drink right now.' Claire suggested we walk down to the Foresters Arms.

The pub was noisy with students behind tankards of frothy beer. We sat in a booth closest to the entrance with our beers and a basket of salt and vinegar chips. I looked across the room and wondered how many of them had been in the crowd today. The news of Steven's arrest would have spread across campus by now.

'What makes me feel sick is that the police went straight for Steven, the only black person in our group at the top of the stairs.'

Andy bit his bottom lip and seemed close to tears.

'When they pushed him to the ground, I closed my eyes.'

Claire slid out of the booth to join him on the other side of the table.

'I won't ever forget the way he looked at me when he was in that cage on the back of the police truck. So bloody calm and defiant,' Andy continued.

Claire slammed the palm of her right hand on the wooden table. 'He needs our help. We are in this together.'

'My older brother is a lawyer, but he's up in Johannesburg. I am not sure whether he can help. I can at least ask him.' Until then I had allowed the two older students to do most of the talking.

Andy and Claire walked with me to a general dealer two blocks away where there was a payphone inside the store. We pooled the silver coins in our pockets. My brother Marcus first sounded a little alarmed to receive a call from me so late in the evening.

Yes, he had seen the footage on the news of what happened on campus but was surprised to hear that I was there at the top of the stairs.

'Rebecca, I am proud of you.'

'I need to ask you a big favour, Marcus.'

I told him about Steven's arrest and asked if he could help.

Marcus offered to contact a partner in the Cape Town office of the law firm. The line started beeping for more money, but we had used up all the coins.

We walked up the hill to the campus where Andy split from Claire and me on his way to the men's residence. We sat down on the concrete steps above the sports grounds so Claire could smoke, close to where our group had gathered the night before.

'What do you think will happen next, Claire?' I watched as she took a long puff from the rolled cigarette, her eyes closed.

'With Steven or with our protest?'

'I am worried about Steven. He is the only one in custody when there were hundreds of us who protested.'

'This is what I think. They will release him with a warning and then we'll continue with the protest.'

I told Claire that I was scared on campus today. 'I am not as confident as you are. Even at school you spoke out against apartheid and injustice in those debates.'

'What happened here this afternoon will be headline news, right across the world. I feel this is our moment.' Claire had reached the last half inch of her cigarette and stamped it out with the rubber heel of her boot.

'I am not saying that I don't want to be part of this, Claire. It's just that I have never been in a confrontation with authorities before.'

◆

It had been two days since the protest on campus. Andy drove Claire and me to the city in his dark green Morris Minor, which was in serious need of a visit to the panel beater. After circling the inner-city block a few times, he reversed it into a tight space on a one-way street.

On our walk to the police headquarters, we passed a boy selling the early afternoon edition of the *Cape Argus*. He wore shorts and an oversized pale blue jersey with the sleeves rolled up to free his hands, barefoot and probably no older than fourteen. He sat with his back against the lamp post; above his head a poster read 'Black Miners Trapped Underground. 6 FEARED DEAD.'

Claire and I had raised 500 rand in cash with the support of our families and a secret door to door collection in the university residences. We waited on the steps outside the brown brick police building while my brother's partner finalised Steven's release on bail.

When the front door opened, the lawyer in his dark double-breasted suit appeared first. Steven followed behind him, wearing the same brown rollneck jersey from two days earlier. A strip of plaster stained with dry blood forced his left eye half closed.

'Thank you for getting me out of here,' Steven said softly. He looked exhausted.

'What have they done to you?' Claire reached out and her fingers touched the side of his face.

Steven didn't respond as he pulled his head away.

I thanked my brother's partner for his help, before we walked back slowly and in silence to where the car was parked three blocks away. An unwashed odour accompanied Steven into Andy's car.

On the freeway out of the city Andy pointed out District Six, an empty strip of land overlooking Table Bay. I knew it was once home to people classified as 'coloured' by the apartheid regime. Only a white-washed mosque stood proud as a reminder of the generations who'd lived in this neighbourhood.

'This place makes one sad and angry.' Next to me on the back seat Claire looked through the window on the bay side of the road.

'I don't really know the full story of District Six.' I felt ignorant but wanted to know more of what happened here.

'The people who lived here were forced to settle on a wasteland, far enough away to make the white people sleep well at night. The last ones were taken away on the back of trucks, like cattle.' Claire's abrupt explanation hung in the air inside the small car.

In the suburb of Observatory, with its rows of semi-detached houses, Andy pulled over at a liquor store where he bought tall bottles of cold beer. We stopped again further down Victoria Road near the hospital; the others waited in the car while I crossed the street to the Groote Schuur Pharmacy. Our last stop on the way back to Rosebank was at a Kentucky Fried Chicken shop.

At the share house Ryan opened the front door and held Steven in a long embrace without saying anything. We moved to the kitchen where Andy opened the beer while I helped Claire to divide the fried chicken with dry bread rolls onto paper plates.

The small curls in Steven's black hair glistened from the shower; I had placed a fresh strip of plaster over yellow antiseptic cream above his left eye. I noticed how he winced when he reached across the table for another bread roll. Andy made him swallow two painkillers with his beer.

In the hours after lunch our group, led by Steven and Claire, discussed what our next plan of action should be.

'Let's not give up now.' Steven was almost pleading with us.

'I agree, this is only the beginning. We won't be silenced so easily.' Claire wiped the mouth of the beer bottle with her thumb before taking another deep sip.

'That's the way, Claire. I've had a few nights in a police cell to think about our next move.'

I thought of mentioning Steven's bail conditions but decided to keep quiet.

It was dark outside when I left the house with Claire and

Andy. Seeing us off at the front door Steven hugged each of us with a repeated, 'Thank you so much.' As Andy steered his car towards Main Road, I touched the back of my neck where Steven had placed his long fingers when we embraced at the front door. I felt a tenderness and thrill that I had never experienced before.

There could be consequences, July 1977

In winter we played hockey on the same field used by the men's cricket team over the summer months. An oval down the hill from the main campus with a white picket fence and a small wooden pavilion with a pitched green roof; tall oak trees around the perimeter were home to an inquisitive squirrel population.

At the end of our midweek practice, I sat down on the bottom row of the pavilion to change my shoes when I noticed Steven just outside the picket fence. He was sitting on the grass with his legs out straight, supported by his arms behind him.

He stood up as I walked closer and gave a little wave.

'Hey, this is a surprise.' I was really pleased to see him.

'Well, my last lecture was cancelled because the professor is sick with flu. I remember you telling Claire about hockey practice on a Wednesday.'

On the far side of the oval was a wooden bench under an old oak that was starting to shed its leaves. We walked across and sat down with my hockey stick leaning on the bench between us.

'How are you feeling now?'

'You mean my ribs?'

'Yes, and your eye, I can see it's still a little bruised.' I was tempted to touch his eyebrow but held my hand at my side.

'Thank you, Rebecca, I feel much better. But do you mind if we don't talk about that today.'

'I was just worried about you, Steven. So, what would you like to talk about?' I hoped he would pick up the teasing tone in my question.

'Okay, I'll tell you a little about myself besides being a law student.' When he reached out, I left my hand on the bench.

'I'm not keen on team sport, but I can run, particularly long distance.'

'Like the marathon?'

'I enjoy the run in the forest, the track from campus to Kirstenbosch Gardens and back. But I don't just jog, I guess I need to be careful, a black man sprinting through the forest can look suspicious around here.'

I smiled but didn't comment.

'Did you compete in athletics at school?'

'Oh, yes, I won the fifteen hundred for seniors, already in my second last year at boarding school. I think it annoyed the older white boys.'

Steven wasn't boasting, he told me about this achievement in a matter-of-fact voice.

I looked up and waved goodbye to three girls in my team as they walked towards the turnstile gate of the hockey field.

'You must have trained really hard,' I said.

'I started running when I was very young, from my first year at school. Our house was more than five kilometres from the farm school. I ran there and back every day with a bag of books on my back.'

It was an awkward moment; a reminder of how far removed my upbringing was from the reality of life across South Africa. I didn't ask another question about his running.

By the time we made our way up the hill the sun had disappeared behind the sharp peaks of the mountain. Outside the front door of my residence students were sitting on the steps in deep conversation. When Steven put his hand on my shoulder my response was very un-Rebecca like. I stood on my toes and my lips touched his cheek.

✦

After breakfast on a cold Sunday morning Claire and I went for a walk in Newlands Forest. We wrapped woollen scarfs around our necks and strode quickly with our hands tucked into the pockets of our jackets. It was damp underfoot and the sun struggled to break through the thick canopy, the air was filled with the sweet scent of fresh pine.

We could hear voices coming towards us, and two students in navy university track suits appeared on the path. When they jogged by, I noticed how the short, stocky guy had an uncomfortable stride as if he was chafing between his legs. It reminded me of Steven's joke about a black man sprinting through the forest.

I waited until we had turned around on the path and started back towards campus before I told Claire that the lawyer had informed Steven the police wouldn't take any further action.

'That's fantastic news, when did he find out?'

'The lawyer phoned him on Friday afternoon.'

'Was that how you heard, from your brother's partner?'

'No, I was at Steven's house when he called.'

When I told Claire that Steven and I had met a few times now, she stopped and looked at me. First with serious eyes, then her face relaxed into a smile, and she put her arm around my shoulder.

'Rebecca, I am excited for you. Steven Mbeki is a guy we all admire. But as a friend, also for the sake of your family, you need to be aware there could be consequences.'

'I feel there is something special between us.'

'All I'm saying is that your relationship will attract attention.'

I knew exactly what she meant; I understood the risk but did not respond. We continued along the path through the forest in silence.

That afternoon I packed a suitcase with winter clothes and my toiletry bag. Walking from the residence, carrying a suitcase, I would have looked like any other student going away for a short break.

On Main Road I hailed a bus on the same route as the first night our group travelled to Rosebank in that storm. There were only three other people on board, all of them white and sitting in the rows closest to the driver. Steven was waiting for me outside the post office and carried my suitcase down the street to his share house.

We hung two dresses and my coat next to his blazer in the narrow free-standing wardrobe. I folded a bath towel on the floor and resting on my knees, I unpacked the rest of my clothes in two neat piles. Steven was right behind me; he bent down and held me without saying a word.

✦

After three days of non-stop rain, driven by a fierce wind that brought down an old tree across our street, we woke on Saturday to a sunny morning with a gentle breeze. The city of Cape Town was washed clean.

Andy came over around mid-morning and suggested a drive to Cape Point. We picked Claire up and she squeezed into the backseat with Ryan and me, while Steven with his longer legs sat next to Andy in the front.

The little car struggled up a winding road with tall trees leaning in from either side. As the only Capetonian in our group Ryan was a useful tour guide. From a gap in the mountain Andy drove through lush farmland; we passed estates at the end of wide gravel driveways, their signboards announcing wine cellars or stud farms. I pointed out that the thatched roofs and white gables were classic examples of what was known as Cape Dutch architecture.

This route took us to the Indian Ocean. The car crawled through beachside villages with names like Fish Hoek and Kalk Bay. As a student from Johannesburg, I felt the excitement of a tourist. Our group's happy mood was boosted further by Ryan leading us in song, he was a Neil Diamond man.

In Simon's Town we passed colonial style, double-storey hotels on the ocean front before we circled around the naval base; then Andy turned left at a sign with an arrow to Boulders Beach. The carpark was empty, and it was an opportunity to stretch our legs after the close to two-hour drive.

From the carpark a sandy footpath snaked through the bush to the beach, we could hear the breaking waves and the noise of squealing seagulls. There was a strong smell of seaweed on the breeze. Steven held my hand as we followed Ryan on the footpath with Claire and Andy closely behind us.

Where the path opened to the beach there was a sign mounted against a wooden pole that read 'WHITES ONLY'.

'Rebecca and I will wait at the car. You guys go ahead.' Steven sounded calm but I could feel his grip tightening.

'No bloody way.' Andy didn't wait for a response as he turned away from the beach.

What started as a fun outing with friends turned into a journey with long silent moments. On approach to the double gates of the Cape Point Reserve where the Indian and Atlantic oceans meet, a large signboard on the driver's side listed conditions of entry in both official languages. Andy made a U-turn without reading the long list.

With a roadmap on our laps in the back of the car we directed him across the narrow Chapman's Peak pass, from where we could see the fishing fleet in Hout Bay harbour. There was no further comment about the sign at Boulders Beach as we took in the spectacular views; the rugged mountains stretching along the Cape Peninsula and the white foam of the waves crashing on rocks below the winding mountain pass. Andy slowed down when three baboons, one with a baby on its back, casually strolled across the road before disappearing into thick bush against the rocky slope.

In the suburb of Sea Point the ocean road made way for hotels and high-rise blocks of flats. I remembered my mother saying this area was popular with the local Jewish community. Andy found parking on the beach front, and it was Claire who spotted an ice-cream counter outside a carousel. From there we walked along a wide promenade. The Atlantic Ocean was still angry after the storm and we watched as big waves rolled towards us before slamming into the seawall, sending a fine mist spray onto our faces.

On a stretch of freshly cut grass there were swings and a bright yellow slide, kids were laughing and screaming with excitement. I stopped to watch a father pushing his daughter, probably three years old in a pink dress, on the swing. The mother, a tall woman under a wide brimmed straw hat, stood close by taking pictures. I thought they were a beautiful family.

Andy and Steven walked ahead towards the light house with its red and white tower. They stopped and I could see Andy pointing to the island visible across Table Bay; the island where political prisoners were locked up for life by the minority white regime.

When we caught up with them, we stood near the seawall licking our ice-creams, until Claire interrupted the silence.

'I wonder whether anybody has ever escaped from there and made it across the bay to the beach.'

Steven laughed and said it was time to go home.

Planning something big, August 1977

On a Friday night around 8.30, almost two months after the first protest on campus, I arrived at Steven's house after our hockey match a little later than usual because the team had celebrated our win with a drink at a popular student pub.

The front door stood wide open, but the house was in complete darkness. Would Steven have gone out without locking the door? I knew that Ryan was visiting his parents on their farm in Elgin for the weekend.

My hand found the light switch in the hallway. It was so quiet I could hear the fridge turn on in the kitchen. I walked slowly through the house, room by room. The beds in both bedrooms were made up; in the kitchen the clean dishes were neatly stacked on the drying rack, the dripping tap still in need of a new washer.

I sat down at the small kitchen table to peel off my long hockey socks. The front door was now locked but I felt uneasy. Did something happen here while I was having a good time at the pub? I thought of taking a shower, but instead I remained at the kitchen table.

My watch showed it was after ten when I heard a car turning in to our narrow street. It stopped near the house, the engine still running. A car door slammed, followed by another, then the roar of the engine as the car pulled away. Silence, the gate squealed and a firm, repeated knock on the front door.

In response to my hesitant 'Who's there?' Steven asked me to please open the door.

There was blood on the front of his grey university

sweatshirt, and he used a handkerchief to stop the bleeding from his nose. He walked straight to the bathroom at the back of the house. I helped him to pull the sweatshirt over his head and he washed his face with cold water.

Steven explained that he had just returned home from his last lecture of the day, and as he closed the gate he noticed a white sedan car parked across the street. By the time he had unlocked the front door three men in suits were inside the gate. Steven asked whether he could help them with anything. The shortest of the three, with a brush cut hairstyle, spoke English with a thick Afrikaans accent. He asked Steven whether he was Steven Mbeki. When Steven nodded, the man placed his right foot in the doorway.

'You're coming with us, Mister Mbeki', and with that the two other men grabbed his arms. He was pushed face down inside the front door before they forced his arms behind his back, followed by the clunk of the steel handcuffs.

'These thugs drove me to a building in the city.'

'The same place where you were released after the first arrest?'

'No, a different one this time; I figured it was the security police headquarters.'

Steven's nose started bleeding again and I fetched a roll of toilet paper from the bathroom.

'We drove through heavy steel gates at the back, and they parked in a courtyard. They pushed me down in a chair, without removing the handcuffs. The room had no windows, just bare cream walls, and a camera above the door.'

Steven and I sat in bean bags with our knees touching as he recalled the interrogation by the security police. The three of them took turns, going back to the same questions in an attempt to unlock a contradiction.

'There was a jug of water on the table, right in front of me. They refilled their glasses, when I asked for a drink, they ignored me.'

I dabbed fresh blood from Steven's upper lip.

'They mentioned Andy several times, suggesting that they knew we were planning what they called "something big" at the university.'

'What did you say?' I hadn't heard about such plans.

'I stuck to my story that a growing number of students, not only at our university, are frustrated that the police were never held accountable for shooting those children in Soweto. This is not a Black man's anger, I told them.'

I snugged up to Steven as he described how the tallest of the officers slapped him across the face. With his arms in handcuffs, he was helpless, just closing his eyes before the next blow on his nose. He felt the blood running down his chin on to his sweatshirt.

Then suddenly it was over. Two of the interrogators grabbed his arms and pulled him up. The shorter one who did most of the talking pushed his index finger on Steven's chest with the promise, 'This is only the beginning.' Still in handcuffs, he was driven back to our house in Rosebank. Not another word was spoken by the three.

'Do you think we should stop the protest, has this become

too dangerous now?'

'Rebecca, how can this be too dangerous when you think about those children? Can you imagine the bravery of a twelve-year-old boy facing up to police with sub-machine guns? They were only protesting, not fighting the police. Let's never forget that.'

Steven held my hands and looked me in the eye.

'These people are coming after us, not because they are powerful, but because they are weak. They are motivated by fear. I could see that in their eyes tonight.'

I wanted to apologise, instead I just kept quiet.

In the silent hours, I lay in bed listening to Steven's rhythmic snoring, occasionally the injury to his nose made him grasp for air. He slept with his back to me; I moved closer to put my arm around him.

I feared the security police wouldn't give up; they had a reputation to uphold. The man next to me in bed was prepared to pay a higher price than I as a white student could understand.

The long weekend, September 1977

I phoned my mother on the Wednesday before the long weekend with the news that I was able to get a lift home to Johannesburg. We'd travel overnight on Friday and drive back to Cape Town on the public holiday on Monday.

'A midterm visit, Rebecca. Your dad will be very excited.'

'I know it's a long way for just a short time, but two guys will share the driving.'

My mother would have known this unexpected trip home wasn't only because I was missing my family, but she didn't say anything.

'I'll invite Marcus and Sarah over on Saturday night,' she said.

I shared the fourteen-hour road trip from Cape Town to Johannesburg with four other students in a light green Volkswagen Kombi with white rimmed tyres. We met mid-afternoon on the Friday in the parking area of a hotel within walking distance from the campus.

The route to the north took us through a mountain pass and at times the Kombi struggled in the lowest gear around sharp bends. In the afternoon sun the mountain streams ran like silver snakes to the river below. Clumps of protea bushes in full bloom decorated the steep slopes.

Beyond the mountains the fruit farms gradually made way for barren landscape as far as I could see. The traffic thinned out to the occasional car passing us at high speed or a truck loaded with sheep heading in the opposite direction for the abattoir in Cape Town.

An elderly couple had pulled over at a roadside stop with a small cement table under a thorn tree, the wife pouring coffee or maybe tea from a flask while her husband stood near the farm fence, peeing with his back to the road.

On a long stretch straight as a pencil, we overtook a cart pulled by two grey donkeys. The dad had a whip to spur on the donkeys; Mum with a red scarf around her head next to him on the bench; the two boys in the back tray, sitting on top of a pile of firewood, waved as we overtook them.

The Kombi slowed as we drove down the main street of Beaufort West, a remote town that became famous as the birthplace of the surgeon who performed the first successful heart transplant. In the darkness, the only sign of life was on a vacant plot of land where men in overalls stood in a tight circle, warming their hands over the fire burning inside a 44-gallon drum.

My mother had reminded me to bring a pillow and so I slept well. I woke at first light as we travelled past the dark shapes of mine dumps on the southern outskirts of Johannesburg. I have come home along this route before, but on this morning, it struck me how the architects of apartheid created their master plan.

On my side of the Kombi, we passed a turn-off to Lenasia, home of the city's Indian population; next I saw two turn-offs, a few kilometres apart, with signboards for Soweto. These were suburbs with residents classified as non-white, thirty kilometres from the high-rises of downtown Johannesburg, hardly visible in the dawn light.

By the time we reached the city the rising sun had a reddish ring around it from the smoke of wood fires and coal stoves in Alexandria, a landscape of small houses and tin shacks without electricity. Home to thousands of migrant workers, the population of Alexandria to the east of the city was a white man's guess.

In the suburbs north of downtown Johannesburg we passed stately two-storey houses behind white walls. There was a warm feeling about being home as we drove along the wide

Jacaranda-lined avenues, with sprinklers on the manicured grass sidewalks.

✦

My mother opened the front door and held me longer than usual in a tight embrace. She was alone at home; Dad had taken the two Labradors for their morning walk around Zoo Lake.

In the kitchen she put on the kettle and arranged the teacups on a tray. I leant against the pantry cupboard and told her that I had moved out of the university residence to a student share house, at least for now. It felt abrupt, but I needed to tell my mother, even before asking about Dad and Marcus.

Mum didn't respond immediately and took a bottle of milk from inside the fridge door. I wondered whether her silence was deliberate, whether this was her message of disapproval. She gestured to the chair on the other side of the kitchen table.

'Is this the Steven guy, are you sharing with him now?'

'Yes, with Steven Mbeki and another student, Ryan Plimsoll.'

In preparing for this conversation on the journey from Cape Town I didn't think of mentioning Ryan.

'Is the house big enough for the three of you?'

'We only have two bedrooms, but it is comfortable. Steven and Ryan are generous housemates.'

'Rebecca, this can become complicated, but you don't have to justify your decision.'

'Thank you, Mum, for understanding. I wanted to tell you first.'

She poured two cups of tea and moved to my side of the

table. I told her about the first meeting at the house Steven shared with Ryan, I elaborated on the protest that led to his arrest and thanked her again for helping with the bail money.

'What happened next, how did this relationship start?'

I sensed Mum was serious in her interest, not just making conversation.

'Steven came to my hockey practice one afternoon; I didn't expect to see him there. After that I went over to their house a few times.'

'Is he older than you, Rebecca?'

'Yes, he is in his fourth year, a law student. He's caring and curious. We can talk for hours.'

I thought about this afterwards, but for some reason I chose not to tell my mother on that day about the security police coming to the Rosebank house, about Steven's second arrest and his interrogation at their headquarters in the city.

Mum and I talked until we heard my father with the dogs at the front door.

When I told Dad at lunchtime that I was sharing a room with Steven Mbeki he first took a long sip from his coffee mug. My father was accomplished at not showing his emotions. He quietly placed his mug on the crocheted placemat and looked at Mum across the table.

It was uncomfortable while I waited for his response. Eventually he stood up and came to stand behind my chair. With his long arms around me he said, 'Rebecca, we love you very much. For God's sake, you must please be careful.'

At that moment I realised they knew all along, even before

my call to say I was coming home for the weekend.

On the journey back to Cape Town we stopped for petrol in the town of Colesberg, a small farming community known for its merino sheep and battles during the Anglo-Boer war. At the service station, I went to the shop for a fruit juice and something to eat. Against the wall next to the entrance there was a sign 'Non-Whites', repeated in Afrikaans, with an arrow pointing to a driveway along the side of the building.

From inside the 'Whites Only' shop I watched as two boys, in their early teens, dropped a handful of copper coins on a latch that opened to the outside. They were just tall enough for their brown eyes to show above the latch. The garage owner counted Sunrise toffees with their distinctive yellow wrapper, two at a time, into a brown paper bag which the boys accepted with a polite, '*Dankie, baas.*'

The brief, but everyday encounter for that part of the world would stay with me always; the subservient tone of their 'thank you', referring to a man to whom they had paid money, most likely earned in return for casual labour, as 'the boss'. The children who faced up to the armed police in Soweto would have been a similar age.

✦

We arrived back in Cape Town late on Monday afternoon. I first went to the residence on campus for a change of clothes and books for the week's lectures. When I moved to the Rosebank house with Steven it was Claire's suggestion that I keep my room in the university residence.

'You never know, Rebecca.'

I found Claire in her room with Andy and two other students. They went quiet when I walked in without knocking first.

'We're just discussing plans for another protest on campus.' Claire sat on a chair at her desk while the others were sitting on her single bed.

Andy added, 'Steven will fill you in on our plans, but this time it will be different.'

Following Steven's last encounter with the security police this casual description of 'different' triggered an alarm but I didn't say anything about it.

✦

Steven greeted me at the front door of the Rosebank house. He held me in a tight embrace and told me he'd missed me very much.

I cooked my mother's chicken curry recipe with naan bread from the Malay family store and we opened a cheap red wine from a co-op in the Stellenbosch district. We didn't talk about our studies, no one mentioned the looming end of year exams, and I didn't say anything about the earlier conversation with Claire and Andy.

'Was it good to be back home, with your family?'

I told him about our family dinner with my brother Marcus and his wife Sarah.

'Marcus was keen to learn more about the protest. They admire you for honouring the sacrifice of the children and standing up to the authorities.'

I was prepared for a question whether my parents approved of our relationship, but Steven didn't ask me.

We were now sharing a bedroom, but I still knew little about Steven's earlier life; only that he was the oldest of four children, he came from a region known as Transkei, that he could run fast, he was at university on a scholarship from a mining company and according to Andy he was a brilliant student.

'Please tell me about your family, about the place where you grew up.'

'Okay, the first thing you should know is that Steven isn't really my name.'

'You're kidding?' I immediately wondered what other surprises this man may be hiding from me.

'Sesethu Mbeki, that's what my parents call me.'

'Does Sesethu have a special meaning?'

'Our gift, that's what it means in Xhosa.'

'I love that, why then change to Steven?'

'It was the headmaster at our school who suggested it. He thought a white boy's name would be better for me later in life.'

I didn't say anything else about his name.

Steven went on to reminisce about a childhood in wide open space, the bitterly cold winters with snow-capped mountains, his memories of men on horseback with woven straw hats and blankets around their shoulders for protection against the icy wind.

'My father is a simple man. I don't mean that he is stupid, just that his life consists of caring for his family, the crop of mealies behind the house and the small herd of cattle that he counts every morning and night.

'I was proud that my father trusted me with the cattle, taking the herd for a day's grazing on the green hills of the Transkei and bringing them back into the kraal before dark.'

'And your ambition to become a lawyer, where did that come from?' I said.

'Going to university was my mother's dream, for me to become a clever man, as she used to say. It was my decision to study law; I thought this is where I can make a difference.'

Steven talked about how the headmaster at the village school, the same man who suggested a white boy's name, persuaded his parents that he should go to a boarding school, four hours by bus along a dirt road from his family home.

In his first year he was one of three Xhosa boys on bursaries at the school.

'I studied very hard; I was determined not to disappoint my mother.'

'I assume all the other boys at the school were white?'

'When I was a young herd boy I didn't care about my black skin, in our part of the world we were all African. It was only when I went to boarding school that that changed.'

'What happened? Was there an incident?'

'Nothing was ever said by the teachers or the other boys, but the three black boys shared a separate smaller dormitory with our own bathroom, and on some of the school excursions we were not included.'

'Did that upset you? Did you and the two other boys ever talk about it or say anything?'

Steven had a habit of biting his left index finger when he was thinking.

'My anger came later; at school I didn't allow anything to get in the way of a best possible matric mark.'

He suddenly changed the subject and asked me to tell him about the road trip to Johannesburg. I chose not to mention the incident I observed with the two boys in the shop in Colesberg. It just didn't seem necessary on this night.

It was late, I was feeling sleepy after the long journey and the red wine. Steven carried me like a baby down the passage to his bedroom, our bedroom.

A matter of state security, October 1977

At the end of their first lecture on a Monday morning, three weeks after the visit to my parents, Steven and Andy were asked to stay behind. The lecturer waited until the other students had left the room before he told them they had been called to a meeting in the vice-chancellor's office.

Andy later described how the secretary with a blonde beehive hairstyle made them wait for at least fifteen minutes. When Steven tried to make conversation with her, he asked whether they were in trouble, she just kept her head down and started banging away on her typewriter. Her phone rang once, and after an abrupt, 'Yes, sir', she led them into a room with dark wood-panelled walls and upright brown leather chairs around a long table.

The vice-chancellor asked them to take a seat while he

remained standing at the head of the table. They had just sat down when there was a knock on the door and three men with hats in their hands walked in, the same three who had taken Steven away for interrogation, now almost two months ago.

The meeting started with the university official, in a stern voice, saying he had learned 'on good authority' of plans for further disruption of lectures. Addressing Steven and Andy as Mister Mbeki and Mister Gibson, he referred to them as the ringleaders. He introduced Major Vlok, the shorter man with the bullneck, before excusing himself from the room.

'The bloodhound who did most of the questioning on the night of my first encounter with the security police then claimed the student protests had become a matter of state security. It was probably not the right response, but I started giggling at this point.' Steven smiled as he recalled this part of the meeting.

Claire and I learnt about this orchestrated encounter with the security police when the four of us caught up in the student cafeteria during the lunch break. We sat at the end of one of the communal tables. Steven and Andy spoke in low voices.

Steven was convinced that the security police suspected a new wave of protests or another form of unrest. 'There is somebody close to us, a person who we've trusted until now, leaking information to the police.'

'Shit, do you really think so?' Claire said, and like her, I was shocked by Steven's accusation.

'I'm convinced those men knew much more than what they disclosed at the meeting. They've managed to get to someone, so let's not discuss any further plans outside this group.'

Steven had been in contact with student leaders on other campuses. The plan was for protests around the country, prior to the exams and spread over two consecutive weeks. Students from these campuses would then travel overnight by bus and train to Cape Town for a mass march on the House of Parliament. Steven predicted a crowd of up to 50,000.

He and Andy left to go to a lecture while Claire and I finished our sandwiches. I watched them walk through the busy cafeteria, Steven laughing with his arm around Andy's shoulder.

✦

My last lecture on a Wednesday finished at 5.30. The mountain had spread its long shadow across the suburbs by the time I arrived at the Rosebank house, expecting to find Steven at home. Instead, it was Ryan who opened the front door.

He was shaking and rambled on about police dogs. Steven had opened the front door, Andy tried to escape over the back fence, a man wearing a hat shouted instructions; they all wore dark hats.

'Ryan, slow down. Tell me what happened here this afternoon.' I had grabbed him by the shoulders and gave him a gentle shake.

'The men pushed Andy and Steven into the back of separate cars.'

'Okay, please start again, Ryan, slowly, right from the beginning.'

Steven and Andy were talking in the kitchen while Ryan was studying in his room. He heard a knock on the front door, then Steven's voice at the door.

'The next moment there were policemen all over the house; some of them in uniform and others in suits. I could hear dogs barking; I saw a dog hanging on to Andy's shirt when he tried to climb over the back fence.'

'And Steven, where was he when they chased after Andy?'

'Already in handcuffs, in the lounge. They went for him first.'

Ryan described how Steven and Andy were pushed into two unmarked cars. Once they were in the cars the men in suits returned to the house.

'They told me to stay in my bedroom while they searched the house.'

In Steven's bedroom the bedding and mattress were on the floor. The drawers of the desk where he studied were pulled out, textbooks and papers had been thrown around the room. Our clothes, including my dresses from the wardrobe, lay in a heap in the one corner.

In the kitchen every cupboard had been unpacked; plates, coffee mugs, canned food, a jar of honey and boxes of cereal were stacked on the counter. The fridge door was open, the ice trays removed from the freezer.

I put my arms around Ryan, and we stood in the kitchen until I could feel he had stopped shaking. We didn't know what to do next, so together and in silence we started cleaning up the house.

Later in the evening I called Claire, and she came over to

stay with us. We didn't think about dinner. Ryan went to his bedroom, but Claire and I spent the night on beanbags in the lounge, waiting, drifting off to a shallow sleep, hoping that there would be a knock on the front door and Steven would be there with his friend Andy.

We felt it was too dangerous to call anyone from Steven's home phone. At first light Claire and I walked to the phone booth outside the post office to call my mother. She asked for the number in the booth and told me to wait there.

When the phone rang about fifteen minutes later, I cried for the first time when I heard my brother Marcus on the line.

'Rebecca, are you on your own at this number?'

'No, my friend Claire Rosen is here with me.'

'That's good. I was just worried that you are dealing with this all alone.'

Marcus asked me to tell him everything I knew about what had happened at the meeting on campus on the Monday and then Ryan's recollection of Andy and Steven's arrest. When I mentioned that the security police had searched the house, Marcus asked whether it was only Steven's bedroom.

'No, they went through the house, even the medicine cupboard in our bathroom.'

'Rebecca, I'll phone you again in two hours, at exactly nine o'clock, on the same number. This time we are dealing with a much more serious situation.'

Claire suggested that we hang around, so we decided to have a cup of tea and a toasted cheese sandwich at a Wimpy restaurant nearby. I stared at myself in a wall mirror above the red fake-leather upholstery of the restaurant. My hair was in a tight ponytail, I hadn't bothered with a shower before we walked up to the post office, there were dark rings under my eyes. Opposite me, Claire had her gaze fixed on her half-eaten sandwich, but I wasn't hungry. The reality of what had happened at our house yesterday closed like long fingers around my throat. I felt vulnerable and scared, like a child. While we sat in the busy restaurant, Steven was somewhere alone in a cell, waiting for the next blow to his face; with handcuffs on, he couldn't defend himself. I wondered whether he'd had anything to eat since yesterday, what was going through his mind right now, what he was expecting us to do, if he thought we could bring him home like after the first protest on campus? Have faith, I whispered to myself, faith in what I hoped for.

◆

A partner in the Cape Town office of the law firm, Jonathan Friedlander, came to the house later that morning. Jonathan was older than Marcus, a slender man with dark bushy eyebrows. He looked at us over his gold-framed glasses and spoke slowly, as if he wanted to be sure that we understood.

Andy was in a cell at the Woodstock police station. Jonathan was uncertain of the exact charge and possible bail conditions. He would get more information from the police but thought there was a chance that Andy could be released later that day.

'Regarding Steven Mbeki, I promise to let you know as soon as I am able to find out where and why Steven is being detained.'

'Should we be worried that they are being held separately?

And only Steven is being held by the security police?'

I was glad Claire asked the question.

'There was no explanation why they were in custody at separate locations. I can only assume the possible charges against them are quite different.'

At the front door the lawyer asked for the phone number at the house. He promised to let us know if there was any further news on Andy or Steven.

'I realise this is a very confronting situation,' he said to the three of us. 'You should not discuss any of the details with other students, at least not until I can obtain more information from the security police.'

✦

I travelled with Claire and Ryan by bus to the Woodstock police station, five stops from Rosebank in the direction of the city. Jonathan Friedlander had phoned earlier that afternoon to say that Andy would be released without bail, the only pending charge would be resisting arrest at the house the previous day.

An officer in a blue uniform behind steel bars, a young man with a centre parting in his straight blond hair, told us to wait in the charge office. We sat on a wooden bench, speaking in low voices, checking our watches. On the opposite wall hung a framed full-colour photograph of the prime minister. The lines in the corners of his mouth made it look as if he had a permanent smirk.

After what felt like an hour, a door opened. A thickset policeman with a pencil moustache led Andy out, holding him by the arm, and then pushed him into the charge office. Andy's corduroy shirt was torn down the front, he carried his shoes with the laces removed in his hand. He dropped his shoes on the floor and the four of us put our arms around one another, until the policeman said it was time to move on.

Once outside Andy immediately asked for news about Steven.

'Oh, Jesus,' he said when I told him that the lawyer was still trying to find out from the security police where and why Steven was being held.

✦

Another two days and long nights with little sleep went by, sharing a bed head to toe with Claire, anxious hours with my face in the pillow, hoping, praying in silence. Jonathan Friedlander called once, only to say that he was waiting for more information from the security police.

Early on the Saturday morning Jonathan, dressed more casually in khaki trousers and a pale blue lounge shirt, came to the house. Ryan and Claire joined us in the kitchen.

'Steven Mbeki has been detained under a new law of ninety days detention without charge. The security police allege he has been planning further, more violent unrest on campus.'

'That's not true, Jonathan,' I shouted. 'Steven is not a violent man, there is no way he would have planned anything we didn't know about.'

Jonathan's face was stern as he held up his hand, and I felt Claire's arm around my shoulder.

'During this time, he'll have limited access to legal representation, but we'll try our best.' He also mentioned that Steven may be transferred to a high security facility.

The next morning the lawyer phoned with an update.

The high security facility turned out to be a police cell in a town ten hours by car from Cape Town. The explanation for the transfer was that it left Steven closer to his family in the Eastern Cape.

Jonathan Friedlander described this as 'very unusual if not suspicious'.

✦

My mother arrived in Cape Town the next day after an overnight train journey from Johannesburg. We shared Steven's bedroom; I couldn't face going back to campus. Mum came with an attitude of hope. Surely the investigation would show that Steven has nothing to answer for. If he was transferred to be closer to his family, perhaps the security police would release him into their care.

Our wait ended just after lunch on Tuesday 12 October when Jonathan arrived without warning at the house in Rosebank.

My mother held my hand, Ryan stood behind us at the kitchen counter. Jonathan took a single sheet of paper out of his brown leather briefcase.

'The security police released this statement a couple of hours ago.'

The lawyer hesitated before he started reading.

'Steven Mbeki died overnight in his police cell in the district of King Williams Town. The cause of death was suicide by hanging.'

I was waiting for more information but that was the end of the statement. Jonathan added that he was deeply sorry to bring this news.

It was silent in the room until I heard my mother say, 'They have murdered him.'

Behind me there was an anguished animal-like scream. Ryan had turned his back to us, leaning with his open palms against the fridge.

I stood up and thanked Jonathan for all he had done, before I walked down the passage to Steven's bedroom and closed the door. His brown wool coat hung on a hook behind the door. I buried my face in the soft fabric, there was the familiar smell of his body.

◆

Claire and Andy came to the house later that afternoon. Andy's eyes were red, his light brown beard showed he hadn't shaved for days. Mum cooked us dinner; we sat around the small round table trying to make sense of this tragedy in our young lives.

With his head down Andy picked at the beef and vegetable stew with his fork. 'Can you imagine how different this would have been if a white student was taken into custody, never to be seen again?'

'It wouldn't have happened Andy, not in this country.'

Claire must have felt uncomfortable about her response and

reached out to put her hand on Andy's bare arm. I looked to my mother behind the kitchen counter, but she had her back to the dinner table.

'It's okay, Claire, I understand and agree with you. Just look at me, here I am tonight, surrounded by friends while Steven lies in a morgue who knows where.'

The rest of our meal remained untouched and we started clearing the table.

'Does anyone have a phone number for Steven's family?' My mother broke the silence.

Ryan said there was a number in Steven's handwriting on the cork board in the passage. The phone was mounted against the wall near the front door.

I dialled the number that said 'Home' and a woman answered immediately. It was the exchange operator in a town called Butterworth.

'I hope you can help me, I'm phoning from Cape Town.'

'Which number can I connect you to?' It sounded as if she wasn't happy to deal with a call at that time of the evening.

'Unfortunately, I don't have a number, but it is the Mbeki family I am looking for.'

'Lady, I don't have such a listing in Butterworth.'

Before I could ask whether she would please make sure the line went dead.

✦

The next morning, with Jonathan's help, I contacted a lawyer in Butterworth, his name was Angus Turner. I introduced myself as a close friend of Steven Mbeki and explained that I was hoping to get a phone number for his family.

Angus Turner called back a day later.

'Miss Kaplan, I was able to speak to Mister Mbeki's mother. The family had been informed of his death and they are waiting for the police to release his body.'

I thanked the lawyer and asked if he could share the number.

'I feel you will be wasting your time. They aren't interested in speaking to anyone,' he said. 'Oh, Miss Kaplan, I should also mention that when I asked whether she was Steven Mbeki's mother she said his name was Sesethu Mbeki.'

I put the phone down without a response.

My mother and Claire packed up my room in the university residence; my clothes fitted into a large suitcase and they put my books with study notes in cardboard boxes. While they were busy packing, I sat on the bed staring through the window at the view across campus to the lush green sports fields below, familiar images that I hoped could be erased forever.

In the days that followed I had no appetite. My mother insisted that I at least drink cups of her herbal tea blend. At night I listened with some envy to Mum's breathing as she slept. I stared at the high ceiling, desperate to go to sleep too, then waiting for the first light of day. I struggled to make sense of what had happened around me, sometimes I wondered whether it happened at all.

Mum assured me that once we were back in Johannesburg, she would use whatever influence possible to find the truth behind Steven's death. I told her that I didn't care, he was gone now.

On the bedside table was a small black-and-white photograph of Steven and me at Ryan's birthday party in the backyard of our house; Steven with a little smile, his elbow resting on my shoulder. I removed the photograph from the silver frame and put it behind the twenty rand note in my leather purse.

✦

The evening of 16 October, not even four months since our first gathering in the student share house, my mother and I boarded the express train for Johannesburg. Andy, Claire and Ryan stood with their arms around one another on the platform outside the open window of our compartment.

'Rebecca, please keep in touch. This can't be farewell.'

Claire remained strong, her chin pushed forward with the usual stubborn optimism, but Andy and Ryan couldn't hold back their tears. There was a last touch of our fingers when we heard the shrill whistle further down the platform.

Once the train pulled out of Cape Town station, I walked down the corridor and found a toilet with a window facing Table Mountain and locked the door. At night powerful spotlights from below lit up the face of the flat top mountain, with the city nestling in its cradle. I bit my bottom lip until I could taste my blood.

Nobody we should trust, November 1977

In our family home I was comforted by flashbacks from my childhood. Mum was diligent in keeping objects of meaning:

my ragdoll in a red dress with two ponytails was on a chair, the pink-and-grey striped blanket she'd knitted was folded across the foot of my bed, on a hook behind the door hung my first pair of satin ballet pumps.

I fought hard not to be dragged down by self-pity. I filled my head with music from a shelf full of cassettes, I stood at the easel for hours, painting abstract shapes with bright primary colours. There were days when I finished a complete novel, it felt as if I had found new meaning in the written word. I lay on the bed and read verses from my personal Hebrew prayerbook, a weekday prayer asking God to look upon our affliction and help us in our need, for the first time I could remember.

In the bottom of my chest of drawers I found a shoebox from the Stuttaford department store with photographs, some in black and white. I sat on the bedroom floor and spread these memories around me on the carpet.

Outside the front gate Elizabeth, our nanny from when I was a toddler through to high school, holds my hand as we walk towards the camera. I remembered the softness of her arms and the fragrance of her soap when she held me in a tight embrace, before wiping my tears with her apron. I knew Elizabeth returned to what she called her homeland and I wondered whether Mum had kept in touch with her, whether she eventually had children of her own.

There was a photograph taken on the beach in Durban during a family holiday. Marcus and I are building a giant sandcastle with spades and buckets, behind us is the lean frame of my father with his unruly blond hair. He watches with hands on his hips. In the background are smart hotels along the Durban beachfront, the photograph shows only white people on the sand.

In my letters to Claire and Andy and Ryan I recalled the late nights we spent bemoaning the evil ingenuity of apartheid; our blind faith after a few bottles of Lion Lager that the protests on campus would lead to the police being held accountable for the murder of the Soweto children. On a lighter note, I asked whether Andy had done something about the sad state of his car. I never referred to Steven in the past tense.

Andy's response came as a shock. I read the letter twice while lying on my bed before I went downstairs, where I found my mother in the family room.

I asked her if I could read the letter out to her, and we sat down together.

"'Rebecca, remember the day when the security police arrived at that meeting in the vice-chancellor's office? Steven said that those men had more information than what they disclosed in the meeting. He suggested there could have been a leak from within our group; a person we trusted who leaked information about the planned march on Parliament. I feel this is more than a coincidence. The week after Steven's death a guy in my residence suddenly disappeared, his name was Herman de Villiers. I'm sure you will remember him, he was also a law student; his father is a diplomat, somewhere in Europe. He didn't say anything to me, but last Friday I heard from one of the lecturers that he had transferred to another university. That was it, no further explanation.'"

'Do you remember the student Andy refers to?' my mother asked.

'Oh, yes, I remember him well. He came to the Rosebank house for some of our meetings. A quiet guy, tall with an unusually long neck, he reminded me of an ostrich.'

My mother smiled briefly, then her face turned serious again.

There was a question I'd wanted to ask since the day my mother and Claire packed up my room in the university residence, but I always pushed it back, for another occasion.

'Mum, I assume the security police know that I had a close relationship with Steven, should I be concerned?'

She looked away to the bay window and nodded.

'A young Jewish woman at an English-speaking university who shared a bedroom with a black activist; the perfect profile to support their conspiracy imagination.'

'Have you discussed this with Marcus?'

'Yes, he agrees with me. Rebecca, we think that outside our immediate family, there is nobody we should trust any more.'

Mum and I sat in silence until I folded up the letter from Andy and walked to my bedroom.

In Claire's letter she wrote that she was nominating for the Student Representative Council next year. 'I am not giving up now. Maybe one day we can make a difference, when justice for all becomes more than a protest chant.'

Ryan gave up the lease of the house before the end of the academic year and decided to leave for London with the help of a British passport on his father's side. In his one-page letter he described Steven as 'the friend I didn't deserve'.

◆

In conversation with family and friends Mum always referred to Steven's death as 'murder'. She contacted our local member representing the white minority party in the national Parliament and managed to secure a meeting for the two of us in this woman's Johannesburg office.

The night before our appointment my parents and I sat around the dining table to prepare our list of discussion points. It was painful to recall the sequence of events in the shadow of that mountain, and Dad kept reminding us to concentrate on the facts.

I woke when it was still dark outside. I felt a tight grip in my stomach, like a teenager on the day of my first exam. I feared I wasn't ready to revisit those final weeks in the Rosebank house, the house that was once such a happy place, the place where I found my voice. At breakfast I couldn't control my tears. Dad suggested that my mother should attend the meeting on her own. I went back to my room.

Mum came home close to midday. She looked tired and asked me to make her a cup of tea. She described the parliamentarian as sympathetic, 'But we shouldn't expect anything to come from the meeting.'

'Although she is a democratically elected member, this poor woman is powerless against a government that uses the security police to do their dirty work. Every sinister action, every time an objector disappears, it is sold to the public as them dealing with a matter of national security. The majority of white people are scared; they believe these fabricated threats.'

We sat in silence until my father said, 'There is only so much we can do.'

✦

Five months after Steven died the head of the security police used the midday news on radio to announce that 'a thorough internal investigation into the death in custody of student activist Steven Mbeki' had been concluded. 'The official cause of death was established as suicide by hanging. The investigation found no suspicious circumstances. The security police consider this case as closed.'

I had just sat down at the kitchen table for lunch with my parents. This was not the major event on the news broadcast, but rather slipped in before the weather update.

My mother leant across and turned off the radio.

'This closes the book on Steven Mbeki's life, perfectly orchestrated on the national news broadcast, no opportunity for further questions.' She spoke with a tired acceptance. 'The people can now get on with life, another threat to white supremacy has been removed.'

I left my parents at the kitchen table and went to lie on my bed with the door closed, the curtains drawn for midday darkness.

In the quiet of my bedroom, I heard a thud, then another, the sickening sound of a skull on a concrete floor. Steven was helpless, his arms behind his back, the cold steel of the handcuffs cutting into his wrists, strong hands pinning him down, the warm breath of a distorted face, shouting, demanding the truth. Steven laughed into this face, he told his interrogator that he looked scared, you are motivated by fear, you are weak, Steven said, you are only acting brave because I cannot defend myself. An angry roar, rough hands with thick fingers around his throat, slamming his head backwards, again and again, the monster stopped only when Steven's body went limp. Then it turned dark in the cell, it was cold on the concrete floor.

Later that afternoon my mother knocked on the door. There was a phone call for me; it was Claire on the line from Cape Town. I told Mum I felt very tired, please tell Claire I would call back later.

✦

My father and I returned to the house from our early morning walk with the dogs, it was a couple of days after the security police announcement.

I closed the front gate while Dad took the Labradors to their water bowl. That is when I noticed a car parked two houses further down the street in the shade of a Jacaranda tree. It was a white sedan with dark windows. When I stopped inside the gate the car started up and drove away slowly in the direction of the city.

At breakfast I mentioned the car to my mother.

'You are no longer safe Rebecca,' was her immediate response.

'What would they want from Rebecca now that they have announced the investigation into Steven's death as closed?' My father sounded surprised by Mum's abrupt verdict.

'The untold chapter behind this tragedy is of the young woman in an intimate relationship with the man they believed was a threat to national security. They couldn't prove anything against Andy Gibson, but they probably think Rebecca was closer to Steven and privy to more information,' my mother said, and pushed her empty teacup to the middle of the table.

There was something I'd wanted to tell my parents about earlier, but I convinced myself it was not serious enough, that it would create unnecessary concern for my family. The car outside our house this morning showed that I was naïve. No, more than that, selfish. On the afternoon when they took Steven and Andy into custody, the security police searched through every room in the house. I found papers from Steven's desk spread across the bedroom floor; when Ryan and I cleaned up afterwards I couldn't find the pages with notes that Steven made a few nights earlier. Notes for the speech he had planned to give at the student march on Parliament. They would have noticed comments or suggestions in another handwriting, my handwriting.

'What type of comment, Rebecca?' Leaning forward, my father rested his elbows on the kitchen table.

'I suggested he should rally the crowd around more aggressive action, that all the talking until then has just been ignored as noise from a liberal minority, "time to raise the temperature", I think was one of my comments.'

In the awkward silence my parents looked at one another. I wanted to apologise for putting my family in this difficult situation, but it felt at that moment we needed silence around the table. My eyes swept from Mum to Dad and back to my mother.

'They are coming after you next, Rebecca,' she said. 'We need to speak to Marcus. I'll ask him to come over this evening, on his way from the office.' This was a situation where my mother stepped up without prompting.

I stood up and rinsed my plate in the sink.

✦

On a midweek afternoon I was reading on my bed. I'd left a gap in the curtains to allow the sun to spread across my bare legs. I heard the doorbell and my mother's footsteps down the passage. There were voices, my mother's and a man, but I couldn't hear the conversation from my bedroom.

The front door closed with a solid thud and then my mother's light tread came towards my room. She opened the door without knocking.

'It was them.'

Mum remained standing next to my bed.

'What did they want?'

'The one who did the talking introduced himself as Captain Van Heerden. When I asked what they wanted from us, he said it was just a routine check.' Mum's breathing was shallow as she told me about the exchange with the security police.

'He then asked whether you live at this address.'

'As if they didn't know already. What did you say, Mum?'

'I told him not to waste my time. The entitled arrogance of these people. He started to walk inside, before asking when you will go back to university. I said it was none of his business.'

My mother sat down on my bed and pulled my face into her shoulder.

✦

By the time the security police announced the investigation into Steven's death was considered 'closed', my immediate family knew I was expecting a baby.

My parents were overjoyed with the news of a first grandchild. Mum wanted to start knitting a blanket and booties. Dad speculated about names; for a girl his first choice was Mum's mother's name Helena or for a boy he liked Ruben. I tried to water down their enthusiasm by saying it was still early days.

During the fifth month of my pregnancy Marcus came over on a Sunday morning. My mother carried a silver tray with a pot of tea, white porcelain cups and a plate of freshly baked scones to the lounge. I waited until we each had a cup of tea.

'Mum, Dad, I have decided to give the baby up for adoption.'

The immediate response was absolute silence. I could hear the ticking of the clock in the hall, before Marcus said that he had contacted an adoption agency with clients in the United Kingdom. The agency had a waiting list of qualified parents on their books.

My father put his cup on the table before he looked across to where Mum sat next to Marcus on the couch. We waited for him to speak first.

'Rebecca, this is a decision with, you know, potentially painful consequences.' He spoke slowly as if he was searching for the appropriate words.

'Dad, I have thought about this carefully, before asking Marcus to help me.'

'I understand, dear, it's just that in my practice there were patients who regretted this decision afterwards, when it was too late.'

'This is not a selfish decision, Dad. This is not about me or us.'

His eyes were fixed on me, but he did not say anything else.

'On the birth certificate our baby will be classified as a non-white person. In this country the child will always be judged by the colour of her or his skin.'

My response hung heavy as my family struggled with our emotions.

'As a single parent, surely only Rebecca can make this decision. She needs our support right now.' Marcus' voice quivered.

My mother stood up from the couch and came to sit on the armrest of my chair.

✦

After Marcus left I went to look for a sunny spot in the back garden. The door to my father's workshop stood wide open. Dad sat on a high swivel chair at his work bench, bent over an incomplete model sailing ship.

Against the wall was a detailed drawing of the ship on graph paper. He was in deep concentration and did not notice me until my shadow crept over his shoulder.

'This is amazing, Dad, such an intricate job. Is this a replica of an actual ship?'

'The Portuguese mariner Diaz sailed this ship around the Cape of Good Hope into the Indian Ocean, almost five hundred years ago. A brave and adventurous fellow, I'd say.' Dad's index finger traced the outline of the ship.

He continued with his work while I watched; with a delicate touch of his long fingers my father attached the small off-white sails to pieces of string or 'sheets', as he called them.

I bent forward to wrap my arms around his shoulders, my face against his neck. He grabbed my elbow with his left hand. I didn't move until he let go of my arm.

✦

Throughout my pregnancy Mum nurtured me with affection and her chicken soup from Grandma's recipe. She joined me for yoga classes in the Jewish community hall; I went on morning walks with Dad to the park with a fountain in the middle of a lake where we did two laps and gentle stretches on the lush green lawn.

Some days the white car was parked across the street. Dad and I didn't bother to give them the usual stare anymore; surely they noticed that I was pregnant. Mum speculated that the security police had the sense to wait, to continue monitoring my next move.

The plans for our baby had been finalised; the adopting parents had signed the required documentation. They were a couple in their mid-thirties from Birmingham in England and planned to arrive two days before my due date. The woman from the agency told me the couple had struggled to fall pregnant and realised it was probably not possible.

Knowing all this in advance seemed to give me some strength to deal with the prospect of not bringing the baby home. My mother's reassurance that 'You're doing the right thing, Rebecca' also helped while I was counting down the days.

Our baby was born in Johannesburg Central Hospital just after sunrise; it was in the first week of June. This date would remain on my personal calendar of family birthdays forever. Mum held my hand during the delivery while Dad waited on a chair right outside the ward.

I was strong enough to be discharged four days after the birth of 'Baby Stevie'. By then she would have been in the care of her parents from England.

A final glance, August 1978

Uncle Simon, my father's younger brother, joined our family dinner this Friday night. When Marcus and his wife Sarah arrived, she gave me a small brown leather-bound notebook with a card; the message inside it read, Rebecca, you are not alone.

The white Ford sedan with two men in the front seat had been parked across the street earlier in the day, my father mentioned. Over the last few months, I'd hardly stepped outside the house, but the security police kept up their vigilance.

Mum had prepared the table with the crocheted tablecloth, and she lit the candles in the two silver candlesticks. I sat in my usual position on Dad's left with my mother on the other side. After Dad's blessing of the challah and wine, a solemn mood settled across the dinner table. Over plates of Mum's fish pie and green beans Uncle Simon and Marcus discussed the route; my brother came up with an estimate of where it would be necessary to stop for petrol.

'Uncle Simon, you probably need to leave here no later than nine, the petrol stations in those country towns normally close by midnight.' As always, Marcus sounded calm and sure of his facts.

I remained silent as my family went over the final plans for my journey into a future I could not see. Mum had planned my luggage down to headache tablets and a second toothbrush. At five minutes to nine she stood up from the table. It was typical of her to manage the farewell in her 'Let's get on with it' manner. My dad sobbed when it was his turn to say goodbye.

In the kitchen Mum handed a basket to Uncle Simon. She showed him the flask of tea with two white porcelain mugs, sandwiches in silver foil and a plastic bag with navel oranges. My parents stayed in the house with Marcus and Sarah when Uncle Simon and I left through the backdoor. From there we could walk behind the hedge into the double garage where he had parked his car.

As we made our way along the streets of Parktown North, Uncle Simon pulled over a couple of times and turned off the lights of his station wagon. Once he was satisfied that we were not being followed he swung onto Jan Smuts Drive and headed north.

On a hill in the suburb of Bryanston I looked over my shoulder for a final glance of Johannesburg. I imagined that I found the cluster of lights where my family were probably still around the dinner table. Uncle Simon asked whether I wanted him to pull over, but I shook my head.

Further north of Bryanston was the newly developed suburb of Fourways. This was where my father first brought me for driving lessons, at a time when streets with empty plots waiting for houses to be built were perfect for a learner driver.

On Sundays a religious group gathered there in the shade of an old Mopane tree with a wide lush canopy; the women wore white and blue dresses with a matching sash and the men dapper in their dark suits. Under Dad's direction, I stopped the car and opened the windows to listen to the hymns, it sounded like a mass choir in a language we didn't understand. I recalled Dad saying that these worshippers would have to find a new place to gather once the white people started building houses in this area.

Beyond Fourways Uncle Simon accelerated the car into a black moonless night on the Highveld. The volume on the music station was turned down low. He concentrated on the road ahead, and didn't make any small talk. He was a bachelor with a record store in Hillbrow, a neighbourhood of flats and night clubs close to the Johannesburg business district. Slightly shorter and chubbier than my father, Uncle Simon was always dressed in blue denims with a t-shirt featuring the world tour of a famous rock band.

I rested my head against the cold window, staring at the dark shapes of trees and telephone poles flying past. I replayed a nightmare that started with Claire's invitation to the meeting at the student share house. Our introduction to Steven Mbeki, the thrill of the first demonstration on campus, packing my suitcase to stay over at the house in Rosebank. Steven's determination to honour the children shot by the police, how bravely he talked after the violent interrogation by the security police. The night Steven carried me down the passage to the bedroom, the news of his murder as my mother called it, her conviction that I was no longer safe. Our baby girl, the persistent presence of a painful memory. The way in which I meekly accepted my journey of no return.

This didn't feel like my life story.

When a roadside sign indicated twenty kilometres to the town of Groot Marico my uncle slowed down and pulled over at a picnic stop. I managed to crouch into the space behind the front passenger seat before he covered me with a folded blanket and started to drive again.

'We are in Groot Marico now,' I heard him say.

After filling up with petrol he stopped again a little way out of town. Once Uncle Simon told me he was sure there were no lights from either direction, I was relieved from my uncomfortable position and moved back to the passenger seat. He said we were now only 110 kilometres from the border.

As our car passed under the steel arc welcoming us to Botswana, Uncle Simon reached over to put his hand on my forearm, but he didn't say anything. It was just after three in the morning when we drove into Gaborone. The streets were deserted except for the red eyes of a brown dog staring into the car's headlights.

Our destination was a white house behind two tall poplar trees. The wooden gates were opened wide and my uncle pulled into the gravel driveway behind a white van. He turned off the headlights but left the engine running. We sat for a couple of minutes; a light flickered on the front porch and then went dark again. A woman in a knee-length dressing gown with a torch in her hand approached our car on the driver's side.

She greeted us with 'Good morning' in what sounded like a British accent.

Uncle Simon leant over and kissed me on my cheek. 'Go well, Rebecca. Remember we love you very much.'

It didn't cross my mind that I would never see my uncle again.

I spent two nights in that house as a guest of Hilda Kenosi, a lawyer educated at Cambridge University, and her husband Seth who worked for the United Nations in Gaborone.

My travel documents for the first leg of my journey prepared by a friend of Marcus's were burnt in the fireplace before Seth handed me a large brown envelope. It was too dangerous to phone my parents as the security police were most likely tapping every call.

At dawn on the second morning Hilda hugged me in the entrance hall and hung a small silver cross on a chain around my neck. With my belongings in a shoulder bag on my lap, Seth drove me to the Gaborone airfield in the white van with UN in large black letters on the door.

He stopped outside a single-storey, grey concrete building; black steel bars protected the windows. He asked me to wait in the van before he got out and disappeared down the side of the building.

While I was on my own, I watched as two armed soldiers in khaki uniforms walked out the front door. I thought they saw me, before they walked away from the UN van. I was relieved when Seth came back a few minutes later.

We drove to a gate with barbed wire on top, where another soldier with a machine gun raised his hand for us to stop. He approached on the driver's side and Seth asked me to hand over the brown envelope. The soldier seemed to read every line of the five-page document with a serious face. Suddenly he smiled and said, 'Miss, I wish you a safe journey.'

Seth pulled away slowly and once we were through the gate, he stopped next to a rainwater tank. We remained in the van until I saw people walking towards a small plane on the tarmac.

'I have your brother's office phone number. I'll phone him later this morning to say you are on your way as planned.' Seth had taken my right hand and held it with both his hands.

'I am very grateful to you and Hilda.'

'Take care, Rebecca, we'll pray for you,' he said before I opened my door.

Seth reversed back through the gate and I watched as he pulled away with a tail of red dust. I waited until I could no longer see his van.

✦

On the eight-seater plane to Salisbury in Rhodesia there were five other passengers and a pilot in civilian clothes. He welcomed us on board and said the expected flying time was two hours. After take-off some passengers started reading magazines, others closed their eyes as we flew in the direction of the sun.

I folded the charcoal jersey my mother knitted, to use as a pillow. I was tired but couldn't fall asleep. From my seat at the window, I looked down on the African bush, grassland interrupted by hills with familiar, sculptured trees and rocky outcrops. To the north white clouds were building up against the clear blue sky; the promise of a thunderstorm later in the day, lightning followed by big drops of rain in the dust, perhaps even hail this time of the year.

When we circled above the Salisbury airport, I could see a large white plane with a red tail in front of the terminal building. At the front and rear of the plane there were flights of stairs with people scurrying up and down. The only other aircraft, in military green colour, was parked a few hundred metres away near an orange windsock.

Our plane made the final approach for landing, I took a deep breath. It felt as if I was adrift on a fast-flowing river, helpless, there was no turning back. As I hurtled towards the promise of a safe place, on the far side of the world, there it was. Just a whisper of hope.

Hear my Heart Whisper

Trapped, in wide-open space
solitude my companion, naked thorn bush, forlorn
scattered across the veld, the riverbed
a dust bowl
hungry lambs, pleading for a feed
on our knees, we prayed, empty eyes
turned to the sky
the raindrops, stayed away

In the stonewalled cemetery, hidden
by poplar trees, slender, leaning with the wind
rest two generations, of my family
wilted flowers, at their feet
one hundred and thirty-two miles, grandpa proclaimed
our nearest village
named after a venomous snake
Pofadder awaited, at the end of this lonely road

Beyond the rocky outcrop, to the south
crouched a scary unknown, of
life, experiences I couldn't imagine
empty stares from faces, who
wouldn't know my name
voices all around me, threatening, in an unfamiliar tongue
feeling small, who could I trust, away
from my mother's embrace, the soothing touch, her
calloused hands

Quiet of darkness, alone, flannel pyjamas, soft on my skin
twisting, restless, what tomorrow may bring
outside my window, piercing
the hoot of an owl
and again, this time closer
ominous, was that a signal, too scared to breathe
I watched, the yellow moon
as it moved away, to that other world

First light, distant glow, in shrill voice
birds rejoice
under my toes, dew on the ground
promise, of a new day, my heart
replenished, a healthy dose, of courage
what if, I dare, to be brave
gentle breeze, cool, licking my face
hope, in my stride

Above, a deep blue dome
the drone of a jet aeroplane, too high
for my naked eye
just a thin white line, painted
with the feather of a bird, across the big sky
where will it swoop, back to earth
way beyond Pofadder
maybe, to that silver city, by the sea

I could hear my heart whisper, not quiver
you are free, go on
explore, where others have wandered, and conquered
in pursuit, of that distant horizon
you may discover
a place of wonder, and miracles
time has come, little bird
for you to fly

My bag is packed, with expectation
toothbrush, holy bible, and
thick woollen socks
the brown envelope, holds
black and white memories, some forgotten
no-one here, to take my hand
first step, cautious
resisting, a glance, at footprints, in the sand.